BRADEN QUINLAN

THE ERRORUNSAI

Contents

Acknowledgement

Thank you, Mom and Dad. This book would not have been possible without your support and encouragement. I appreciate the countless nights and weekends that my Dad spent preparing my first book for publication. Thank you also to Parker, Aunt JoAnn, and Uncle Roy for the feedback that you provided to make my book even better.

1

The Rise of the Revolution

"I am not about to go up to that tyrant's guards and let them send me to a dungeon," Joseph told his mother Margaret.

"It will be okay. They won't torture you. They are not monsters."

Joseph hung posters that insulted King Salo. While her son thought King Salo was a tyrant, Margaret firmly believed the King of Sorwond, Salo, was a great king. Joseph was angry that the king taxed the people daily. The king's guards took you to the courthouse if you could not pay the tax. Most people who went to the courthouse never came back, and the names of those "criminals" were forbidden to be spoken, even by family.

Why did Joseph believe that the people who could not pay the tax were not really criminals? Because the tax was impossible to pay. To access the mine or logging camp and earn coins to pay for the tax, one must pay an entrance fee. For the logging camp, the fee is a ten-foot-long log, which you can't get unless you had access to the camp. The fee was ten pounds of stone or ten pounds of iron to access those mines. A similar story applied there, too.

Why was Joseph's mother faithful to King Salo? Because she attended the speeches by the king. The king manipulated people with his speeches, and it was mandatory to attend them. However, Joseph hid in the attic during the speeches, each time escaping the guards' search of the houses during this speech. Although the guards could not see him, he watched the guards through a crack in the attic floorboards. During one search, he witnessed a guard steal a gold coin! Because of her faithfulness, Margaret insisted that she and Joseph lost the coin.

"They are monsters. I can name a few relatives who were dragged away for not being able to pay the tax. Now, since it is illegal to remember the relatives that tyrant murdered, I won't name them," raged Joseph.

"That is all! You are banished from this house!" Margaret yelled.

"Then so be it. I will go and start a revolution. Sorwond's current government cannot stand!" Joseph packed his sword, bow, axe, pickaxe, chain mail shirt, and resource backpack. Unfortunately, he had no arrows for his bow, but if he got some, they would come in handy. He left the house and went to the gate, which, as always, was closed. Step one was to escape the kingdom, so he could find other escapees and start this revolution.

Joseph knew his axe would be useful. He found a secondary gate, which a guard watched from atop the five-foot-thick wall that surrounded the Kingdom of Sorwond. The gate was wooden and Joseph chopped through the wood. It had stone bricks on the other side, probably to make it blend in with the rest of the wall.

"Rebel!" shouted the guard. The guard put down his spear and picked up a bow. Next, he picked up an arrow and knocked it into his bow. He pulled the bowstring and aimed for Joseph's head. The guard missed. Joseph picked up the arrow and pulled his bow from his backpack. Joseph did not miss when he fired. The guard was dead. Joseph used his pickaxe to break through the stone brick part of the gate and freed himself. He ran into the woods and hid for a night, sleeping on the grass.

The next day, Joseph crafted a hammer and some wooden nails, and built a shelter with the little wood he had. He also chopped more wood with the axe he brought. He found a small river for drinking water. There were some cows around, so he made a pen for them. He could farm them after they had some offspring. He set up a tent with wool from wild sheep. Now, he had a functioning shelter.

So far, the soldiers of Sorwond didn't seem to be looking for him in the wild. They must still had been searching the kingdom. Joseph went on another wood-chopping expedition and made basic battlements to defend himself, such as a wall and lockable door. He used flowers to make dye to blend the wool into the environment, preventing the guards from seeing him from their perch on the kingdom's walls. He designated a mining area and left his pickaxe on a wooden rack there. He hung his axe on another rack near the door that served as the gate for his small fort. Since he planned on raising a rebel militia against Sorwond, Joseph cleared room for more tents or even small houses. He prepared an area for a dining hall, armory, blacksmith, storage room, and bank. He planned on using Sorwond coins, as that would be what any escapees were likely carrying. He was ready. Now, he just needed a few rebels to get this going. Joseph decided to call this place the "old fort." It was not old, but it felt so because of the long hours of work it took to make.

A day later, Joseph observed a figure in the woods. He took

his sword and approached the figure. It was another escapee! He carried Sorwond coins and some basic tools.

"Greetings. My name is Joseph. I am attempting to start a revolution against Sorwond. I have a camp with a reliable food and water supply. There is room for another tent or a house, if you would join me."

"So, totally normal for someone to approach you and invite you to their militia, is it? I would join, but how soon do you plan on attacking? I want to make sure I am not dealing with an insane man here," the escapee replied.

"When I have enough men, I might have some of them kill a few guards and keep our enemies busy. Don't worry. For now, I am trying to find a comrade."

"I'm in. My name is Thomas, and I have a sword, bow, spear, axe, pickaxe, hoe, shovel, water, food, and a shield."

"Well, we could use a good amount of those things. Let's start a revolution."

2

Fight, Flight, or Sleight

"Klokar, we saw humans in the woods. They built a fort and were drinking water from the Sacred River," a centaur reported.

"Do not kill them. They don't seem to know that these woods are that of the centaurs. I will make sure they know, personally. Deliver this note to the gate of their fort," instructed Klokar, the king of centaurs.

"Yes, Klokar."

Joseph and Thomas returned home from the woods. There was a note on the door to their fort.

"Huh?" Thomas uttered.

"Let me read it," Joseph said, grabbing the note.

The note read, "These are the Centaur Woods. You are unwanted here. War or peace is your choice. Leave, and you get peace. Stay, and you make war. These woods belong to the centaurs. Whether or not you wish to fight this mighty race is your choice. Half-horse, half-man, we traverse this terrain quickly. Swift will be your demise, should you choose to stay."

"Disturbing, very disturbing," Thomas said. "I heard of centaurs before. They are, like the note stated, half-horse, half-man. Where the horse's head and neck end, the torso of a human begins. They are as fast as horses and as skilled in combat as a Sorwondian knight. We don't stand a chance fighting them. We either move, die, or try to reason with them. However, reasoning with them is just as risky as jumping off a cliff."

"Mighty Klokar, the note was delivered," the centaur announced.

"Very well. Monitor them for the next week. If they aren't gone from the woods, bring them to me so we may prepare a feast...," Klokar declared, "out of them." Klokar sent a centaur to watch the fort from a cave on a small hill, armed with a centaur longspear.

"So, fight or flight? What do you think?" Joseph asked.

Thomas replied, "I would say fight if we had more men, but we don't. We put a lot of work into this place, so flight does not seem like a good idea either."

"What if we pretended flight, but really stayed. We can hide our valuables in a cave. I think there is one in that hill over there. Then, we construct a hidden base in that cave with a secret door in the back of the cave. If centaurs spot us, we will run into the cave and into our base, and shut the door. They would have no idea we are there and assumed we used a potion to become invisible or something," Joseph said.

"Yeah! That would be...sleight?"

"I guess so. Well, let's get moving. We don't know how long before centaurs come back."

The next day, Joseph and Thomas went to the cave. A centaur was there to greet them.

"What is that?" Joseph questioned.

"Kill it!" Thomas screamed.

Soon they were in a melee fight. The centaur tried to stab Thomas, and failed, allowing Joseph to slice his human part off his horse part, killing the centaur. Joseph and Thomas buried the centaur under the floor of the cave. As planned, they made the secret door with a small room behind it, and moved in.

"That was a centaur," Thomas said.

"Well, we have a fight on our hands!" Joseph exclaimed.

Joseph made a peephole in the cave that was angled towards the sky so they could tell the time. They covered the outside of the peephole with leaves and shrubs. Thomas had stolen some ingredients on his way out of Sorwond and managed to make a potion that gave off light. It would never run out because the liquid was simply glowing. It didn't destroy itself in the process like a torch or campfire. The only problem was that it is corrosive to anything living.

"Why does it have to be corrosive to life, again?" Joseph asked.

"For the thousandth time, the ingredient that makes it corrosive is the one that makes it glow. If we want light, we must deal with the corrosiveness." Thomas groaned as Joseph moved on from that conversation and began mining because they needed more stone. "Be careful to not make another opening. Fortifying one entrance is enough." Thomas then asked, "Should I go woodcutting, or should I mine with you?"

"Stay here. We cannot afford to split up now. It is too dangerous to go alone."

Together, they mined until they noticed through their leaf-covered peephole that it was time to get some shut-eye. When they awoke, they looked through the peephole to make sure it was day, and together went woodcutting. Upon returning, they stacked the wood in the corner of the cave. Next, they expanded their base and made a separate storage room. They made plans for a dining hall, barracks, document storage room, designated place to mine, potion brewing room, melee training room, shooting range, a head overseer's office for Joseph, four offices for each of the overseers Joseph planned to have, one of them being Thomas, a workshop, a blacksmith area, rallying room, a huge armory, and a ladder that extended to the top of the hill for a future watchtower. Of course, they also had to make a really long hallway to allow for these plans. After a long day of mining and woodcutting, they got more shut-eye.

The next day, Joseph and Thomas decided to name their rebel faction. They named themselves the Rebellion of Broken Chains. They also made a wool banner for the faction and added a banner station to their plans. Afterward, they went looking for escapees and gained fourteen rebels! Apparently, there was a jailbreak back at Sorwond. The prison was square, and two of the four prison walls were also part of the wall surrounding the kingdom. The lucky prisoners managed to break through one of the prison walls that also surrounds the kingdom. They snuck pickaxes into their cells from the mines that they were forced to mine. All fourteen escapees had cells along the outside wall. A guard fell asleep one day and forgot to walk by everyone's cells. They mined themselves out of prison. The new rebels told of being attached to torture machines, witnessing the killing of fellow prisoners because their uniforms were ripped from slaving in the mines or because they had pebbles in their shoes. After the addition of the fourteen rebels, Joseph and Thomas added a medical center to their plans, right next to the potion shop. They made the potion shop a reality and healed the wounded rebels in there until they were able to build the medical center. The rebels got to work making the base, mining for the whole next week. None of the fourteen could be happier mining in this cave, for they were now free. They also were going to kick the Sorwondians' butts.

By the next week, the rebels constructed most of the rooms. They would have to expand the barracks and dining hall when they got more men, but for now it was of sufficient size. They built one overseer's office since only one overseer was identified. In time, Joseph would have to promote the rebels that seemed best for the role for the other three positions. The head overseer's office was ready, though. Joseph sent five men to cut trees and hunt for escapees, five to mine, and the other five he told to relax. Each group swapped assignments, and after a while, they swapped again. Joseph oversaw the groups. Everyone got a chance to relax, mine, and cut trees and hunt for escapees. That was how it was going to go for the next few months. New escapees would be equally distributed among the groups.

"Wake up! Wake up! Wild barbarians are here! They are in the cave entrance and one has a pickaxe. They seem to want to set up camp in the cave. Chances are they are going to mine towards us," a rebel announced to the others in the base.

Soon all sixteen of the rebels were in the entry area, waiting for the right time to charge into the cave and kill the barbarians.

"I think there are three. I only hear three different voices," a rebel whispered.

"Three, two, one, CHARGE!!!" Joseph shouted.

They unlocked the secret door, opened it, and began fighting. There were, in fact, three barbarians. One had two small hatchets. Another barbarian had a bow and a quiver of arrows. The third put down his pickaxe and picked up a mace. One of the rebels shot the barbarian with the hatchets in the left arm, giving another rebel time to decapitate the dual-wielder with a cleaver. The archer barbarian got off a shot and struck one rebel's right knee, who was dragged into the rebel hideout by another rebel. This left two barbarians and fourteen rebels in the fight. One rebel screamed and knocked the archer barbarian's head off with a mace. The remaining barbarian with the mace was on a kill streak. He rushed two rebels, decapitating one and wounding the other. Then, the same rebel who shot the first barbarian, shot the rusher in the back of the head and killed the final barbarian. The rebels discarded the three bodies into the river near the old fort. They disposed of the campfire and tents the barbarians were setting up, too. The rebels went inside to get a status of everyone. Both wounded rebels survived their wounds and were healed with potions. They buried the one rebel who died in a new room, the burial room. The rebels inscribed his name and an outline of his body on the wall so he was not accidentally dug up. They had a proper funeral, and then left him to his rest.

The rebel who shot the first barbarian and got the final kill became an overseer. His name was Bill, and Thomas observed that they would need a chain of command as new overseers were identified. Thomas thought orderals should report to an overseer and that there should be four orderals to one overseer. Joseph liked the idea, but said the new chain of command should wait until more men joined the faction. Thomas agreed and instructed a rebel to document this new command structure. Another rebel documented the violent battle. They placed both documents in the document storage room. The remaining rebels went on patrols and found three more escapees. People were happy about that. Their numbers were growing.

As time passed, one of the centaurs reported back to Klokar.

"Klokar, I am suspicious that the humans did not leave. We were unable to find any footprints in the dirt leading out of the woods. Also, the centaur watching the fort did not return and no report came back from him."

"No report means the humans are gone and the watchman is roaming the woods, living in our mighty realm," Klokar insisted.

"Very well, Klokar. You eased my concern." With that, the centaur left Klokar to his thoughts.

3

Gathering Arms

"Overseer Thomas, send some rebels to spy on Sorwond. Now is the time to see what is going through the King's mind," Joseph declared.

"By your command." Thomas sent three spies, and this is what they saw.

"Greetings! Greetings! Hello my people. The daily tax was collected, and there are a few violators of our laws. How terrible! People refuse to pay a small tax to their king. I use the money collected to build homes for them! I make barracks for the military to defend them! This is not acceptable," Salo complained.

"You want to know what is unacceptable? Some of us wish to leave to see others. The houses you build are too expensive. The tax goes towards military buildings for guards that enforce tyranny or a palace for our 'great' king! You use sorcery to make your speeches manipulate others!" shouted a teenage citizen in the crowd.

A guard shot the teenage citizen with a bow right after he finished speaking. Some citizens started crying or gasping, while others ran. A riot control team killed all runaways, and royal enforcers killed sobbing relatives.

"Citizens! Why would you want to leave?" Salo questioned. All the citizens instantly stopped and listened. "Why can't you afford a house? I am sure you are all very wealthy. The tax is little, and you all know how much the guards do for us. The speech is ended! Go, go and serve your kingdom!"

"It is amazing," one of the spies said, "how they all just listen. I guess it takes time for the sorcery in the speeches to work. They have to attend a few speeches before the king can control everyone like that. I guess that teenager and his relatives were new."

"I know," another spy said. "This is what we have to end. This is what the Rebels of the Broken Chain fight for."

Upon their return to the base, the spies prepared a report of their observations.

"We got the report from the spies, sir and it isn't good. Here it is," Bill said.

Joseph was frantic. "He turned into even more of a tyrant, and his sorcery got stronger! We must fight now! We need to free the citizens! No, we need more rebels and be better prepared for the fight. We must wait." Although conflicted, Joseph calmed down and resumed his job of head overseer.

Joseph summoned Thomas and Bill to his office one afternoon. "Welcome, overseers. Today, I called you to a meeting regarding Centaur Woods and the centaurs. As you know, we are on their land, and we hid our base for that reason. One of the rebels learned that the name of the centaur king is Klokar, and he wields a heavy axe. He and his bloodline, unlike the other centaurs, have horns. I now know where his throne is, which is where he spends most of his time. We need to conduct an operation to destroy Klokar and his bloodline, leaving the centaur race in chaos."

Thomas responded, "How do we plan to do this? An inside man won't work, since we are not centaurs."

"We will use a siege engine to put a boulder on Klokar's head," Joseph said.

Bill then asked, "How do we get a catapult anywhere near the palace without anyone noticing?"

Joseph had the answer. "I made a potion we can rub into our materials that will make the materials invisible to centaurs. Because the potion does not make things invisible to us, we will need to first test it with a centaur."

Thomas jumped back into the conversation. "We can use the potion to make ourselves invisible by rubbing it onto our clothing. Or we could test it on a smaller scale by placing a sign that says 'Klokar is garbage!' on top of the palace's gate. If it is still there the next day, we know the centaurs can't see it."

After the meeting, the overseers devised a plan they put into action. They decided to place a dummy raider about thirty yards from the palace gate in a tree. A three-man rebel team equipped the dummy with black-dyed cloth gloves, pants, and leather shoes. They added a hood for the head, dyed red so if the centaurs could see it, they would surely notice it. They placed a wooden bow in the dummy's one hand and an arrow in the other hand, as if the dummy was about to knock an arrow and draw the bowstring. The dummy had a quiver full of sticks on its back to look like a quiver of arrows. All items on the dummy were rubbed in the potion that made objects invisible to centaurs, and the dummy raider was put into position. Satisfied with the job, the rebel team returned and reported their success to the head overseer. "We positioned the dummy thirty yards away from the main gate of Klokar's palace, sir," reported the commander of the three-man team. "The centaurs did not see us or the dummy. The potion-rubbed clothes we wore seemed to work as none of the centaurs came close to us or looked in our direction."

"Mighty Klokar, we spotted footprints in the woods. They lead towards the fort built a while back, but after about sixty yards they disappear. This concerns the elders and me. I urged you before, and I urge you again, Sire, release the centaurs to search for the humans. The footprints prove they are still here," Klokar's servant urged.

"You convinced me. Search every possible location in the woods, even those that have already been checked," Klokar instructed.

The next day, Thomas called Joseph and Bill to his office for an emergency meeting.

"What is going on? Why are we meeting in your office, Thomas?" Joseph asked.

Thomas explained, "There are centaurs roaming throughout the woods. They seem to be looking for something. I believe they know we are still here."

"The report stated that the team went unseen. However, the centaurs must have spotted something else, such as footprints," Joseph said.

"If that is the case, then the potion works. We can walk through the woods unseen," Bill replied.

Joseph called the three-man team to his office and told them to check on the dummy. The team departed and found the dummy was untouched. However, they discovered footprints they made during their previous trip. "Pat the ground down behind us. We must cover our trail on our return!" directed the commander. Upon reporting back to the fort, the commander told Joseph, "Sir, we determined the reason that the centaurs are patrolling the woods. We observed footprints that led to a point about halfway between here and Klokar's palace. Luckily, the footprints made it look like we were headed toward Sorwond."

After the report from the commander, Joseph assembled a meeting with the other two overseers to exchange status updates. "Thomas, begin with your information."

"Well, there isn't much. Just some numbers on resources that we gathered. Unfortunately, no new escapees," Thomas reported.

Next, Bill provided an update, "Similar story to Thomas, except we gathered lots of stone. I figured we would need it for a forge."

After Bill finished, Joseph told them about the discovered footprints. He told them that centaurs were on the hunt for the rebels. "Luckily, none of the centaurs found our secret entrance in the cave. Because of this setback, I suggest we remove the commander of the team. The commander should have known better and has put all rebels at risk. We should release him to the wilderness, with him taking only what is his."

Thomas countered, "While I agree with the reasoning, I think we should execute him. Otherwise, he might turn over information to the centaurs, or worse, Sorwond. We should construct a prison and execution area."

Bill suggested, "Well, if we have a prison, maybe it would be better to throw him in there for a while before we consider execution." Thomas and Joseph agreed with Bill's suggestion.

The team commander walked through the main hallway and headed to the cafeteria for lunch. He hoped that high command wasn't mad about the footprints. He entered the cafeteria, ordered his food, and sat down. The commander had a table with his team in the corner, and only the team could sit there.

"Halt!" ordered a stern voice behind him. When he turned around, he saw the head overseer with the two other overseers beside him. The commander now knew that the overseers were mad about the footprints. "We must confiscate your armor, weapons, clothing, torches, personal items, and any weapons. You are being detained for failure to hide tracks and exposing the location of our base," declared a rebel escorting the high command trio.

"What? I did not do it on purpose!" the desperate commander exclaimed.

"It does not matter. You exposed our position. Now, hand over your armor," Thomas instructed.

The commander changed into thin cloth shorts and a white armband that covered his entire right arm. A rebel took him to a desk in the cellblock, which was constructed while he was doing his morning duty. Right now, there was only one small cell, obviously meant for him. Floor-to-ceiling stone columns prevented him from escaping, but allowed him to be watched.

"What is your name?" asked the rebel behind the desk.

"Kevin," replied the former commander and now the first prisoner.

"Your prisoner ID is 0001A." The rebel then opened the big stone door and forcefully threw Kevin into the cell. The rebel closed the door and slid the deadbolt into the lock position.

Kevin did not yet know that the prison ID was basically his name now. He found that out at breakfast.

"0001A, we have your rations," a rebel announced.

"Sir, my name is Kevin."

"Say that again," taunted the rebel, grabbing a leather whip the warden gave him.

"Sorry, sir," apologized Kevin.

The rebel left without giving him breakfast. That was prison life. It was sort of like life in Sorwond, just without the torture. At least the rebels here had a reason to lock him in a prison cell. Joseph jailed Kevin to set an example for the rebellion. The commander messed up and would be detained for ten years. Although a harsh punishment, Joseph knew Kevin would at least get three full meals a day, unless he disrespects the guards who deliver them. It seemed like a fitting punishment.

Later that day, Thomas entered Joseph's office and told him that there were centaurs in the entry cave.

"Make sure the door is locked. Let them search. Don't attack unless they enter our actual base," Joseph instructed. Joseph left his office so that he could observe for himself. When Joseph arrived near the entry cave, the panicking rebels calmed down. The rebels had propped wooden poles against the door in case the centaurs attempted to ram it down. "Soldiers," Joseph whispered, "do not attack unless they realize we are here. If one search party dies, and the others do not, it will be very suspicious. If we must attack, we must also attack the other search parties to prevent them from guessing our position and returning with siege engines."

The rebels whispered their agreement. Soon the centaurs left and returned to Klokar's palace. After the centaurs left, Joseph ordered the rebels to get the potions ready and make more clothes and wood invisible. Joseph told them that they would soon start an invisible strike on the centaurs. The rebels rushed around to prepare the items. Once the items were ready, the rebels organized for a march to Klokar's palace.

"Mighty Klokar, we searched throughout the woods and

checked the wooden fort that the other humans left. We failed to find the humans," the centaur servant reported.

Klokar screamed, "I want them kneeling before me in a week, or your head will be on a shelf somewhere in this palace!"

"Yes, Sire!" The servant left the throne chamber, knowing he had to find at least one human to please Klokar.

A week passed and no humans were found. "I beg you, Sire!" the servant cried. He was standing on a platform in the execution room, with his head through a wooden board with a hole in it.

"You failed me," Klokar scoffed, holding the lever that would drop a large blade roped to the ceiling right onto his neck. Klokar pushed the lever down a bit.

"If you will not let me live, make it swift," the servant begged.

"I can grant that request, for sure." Klokar pushed the lever all the way down. Two guards quietly brought the head and body off the platform while Klokar warned his army. "The execution is ended. Know not to fail your king, and you will not end up on this stage with me." Klokar called for another servant and remarked, "I will be merciful to you, since you are new. The humans are hiding. You need to find them. It is simple hide and seek, except there are a lot more seekers than hiders. Now, go!"

As Klokar made the importance of finding the rebels known to the centaurs, the rebels began their march through the Centaur Woods and on the way to Klokar's palace. This time, those in the back patted down footprints. "Centaurs ahead," whispered the rebel at the head of the march. Everyone stopped marching. They had just stumbled upon another search party patrolling the woods. This was the fifteenth search party that the rebels encountered, and they weren't even halfway to the palace. The pace of the march would certainly be slow.

4

Struggle for the Centaur Woods

"Great One, we located some human rebels with strong potential. They are rebelling against Sorwond, but are currently trying to gain control of Centaur Woods," reported a soldier in armor of black steel, with a spear of the same steel and a spearhead of yellow mist. The soldier had a helmet with a visor covered in the same yellow mist and a frontal spike of this strange yellow mist.

"Very well. Send an army to the woods and see if we can assist them," said the leader of these black steel armored soldiers. "I suspect they have a means of invisibility. Otherwise, they would never march in that direction. Centaur patrols should have had them in their sight many times along their route."

The Rebellion of Broken Chains marched through the woods undetected. Soon they were in position and began constructing the catapult. As they built the catapult, figures in black steel armor holding black spears with tips of...it didn't matter, appeared and looked as if they were there to slay the rebels.

"What do you seek?" Joseph asked the figures. A few of the figures had bows and a quiver filled with the same yellow mist that formed the spearheads of the spearmen. Joseph noticed that this mist also covered the visors of the men's helmets and the bow limbs were made of black steel.

One bowman pulled an arrow from the quiver and held it in his hand. The tip was covered in the glowing yellow mist. "We, too, seek the demise of Klokar and Sorwond," all of these soldiers declared at once.

Joseph replied, "I don't know where you're from, but is it normal to surround somebody with soldiers, point spears at them, and then ask to be allies?"

The black steel armored soldiers told Joseph that they were from Edhormon. "We come from Mount Edhormon and serve one leader. He brought to life the stone we are composed of, and we serve his greatness. He willed for the demise of Klokar and Sorwond as do you. Therefore, you either accept our alliance and kill our mutual enemies together, remain neutral and fight on your own as we watch you bleed, or declare war on us and be destroyed. Out of your options, allying with us is your best choice."

Thomas challenged the soldiers. "If we agree to fight alongside you, you will need to prove to us that you won't use your spears to stab us in the back."

The soldiers replied in unison. "We have no intention to prove our allegiance. You can either trust us or not. The choice is yours."

The rebels agreed that teaming with the new soldiers was their best option, but Bill had one request. "It is kind of creepy how you all talk at the same time. Could you talk one at a time?"

The rebels now had the spearmen on their side, increasing their ability to fight. Together they struck Klokar's base. The strike on Klokar's palace went relatively successful, either injuring or killing Klokar and destroying his throne room. The joint rebel and Edhormond team surprised the centaurs. A few centaurs saw the Edhormond spearmen approaching, but the attackers stabbed the centaurs before they could report the Edhormond presence. Not fully trusting the Edhormond, Joseph assigned two rebel soldiers in heavy armor to watch them overnight. The rebels made the interesting discovery that the Edhormond did not sleep. They also didn't have to eat, drink, be entertained, or need a break from war or work. The Edhormond were devoted entirely to war. The rebels also found that the Edhormond did not know how to cut wood. Rather, they only knew how to forge with their Edhormond steel and mine stone. The Edhormond told the rebels that, back home, they mined stone and chiseled stone blocks into the shape of the Edhormond soldiers. Then, the Edhormond leader brought the body to life and the new soldier was equipped and sent to war.

Away from the battle, a meeting took place. "How did the engagement with the rebels go?" asked the Edhrine, ruler of Mount Edhormon.

"Very well," his second-in-command reported. "I watched from a distance. We now know the location of the rebel base. My stalking abilities served me well and I found the entrance. I suggest that now is a good time to launch a siege on Klokar's palace. The recent attack may have left Klokar dead, but we can finish his bloodline and drive the centaurs' evil race to extinction."

"Now is a good time, indeed," the Edhrine agreed. "Launch the siege. Let the first dream of the rebels come true, before we unlock the true potential of these humans."

"Sir, the Edhormond are gathered by the entry cave. They say it is time to siege Klokar," a rebel reported to Joseph.

"Are they insane? Any sane man...or...stone thing would not go to war with our current numbers."

"They say their 'brothers' await."

"Let them go and die without us, if that is what they wish."

At that moment, an Edhormond spearman atop one of the Edhormond siege towers shouted, "Klokar's realm will not stand! For the Edhrine!"

"For the Edhrine!"   the hundreds of other Edhormond shouted in reply.

"Charge!" shouted the Edhormond commander of the siege. The Edhormond spearmen brought a black steel battering ram into position, while the Edhormond archers in the siege towers targeted the centaur archers.

Soon, an army of centaurs came out the gate to destroy the battering ram.

"Berserkers!" yelled the siege commander. Once called, massive Edhormond soldiers wearing only helmets advanced with massive spiked shields and cleavers. The stone berserkers charged the army of centaurs and defeated them within minutes. After the battering ram was in place, a berserker pushed it straight into the centaurs' gate. One push shattered the gate into a million pieces. Edhormond spearmen rushed through the gate and engaged centaurs stationed throughout the palace and made their way to the throne room to determine whether Klokar was dead. The berserkers stayed outside to make sure no centaurs escaped.

"Klokar! Are you in there?" a centaur servant yelled. Klokar was in the throne room when it collapsed during the attack. After a long search, the centaurs found Klokar buried in the rubble. Rubble impaled him in many places and he was dead.

"No! Klokar is dead!" the servant screamed. "But that means I will now reign," thought the servant. Klokar's mighty axe was beside him, stuck in the rubble. The servant pulled on the axe, concentrating his whole mind and body to free the axe. He heard noise behind him, but he didn't let that distract him. With the axe, he would rule over the centaurs.

"I have a feeling those spearmen aren't dead yet," Joseph said to Thomas and Bill.

"What are we waiting for? Let's check on 'em," Bill responded.

When the trio arrived, huge stone berserkers greeted them. There were also a few spearmen sitting outside waiting for those still inside. They spoke with the siege commander and learned everything about the siege. Joseph, Thomas, and Bill entered the gate, with rebels in tow, and encountered numerous dead centaurs. The rebels came upon the bulk of the siege party, headed for the execution and throne rooms. The high command trio went toward the throne room and the rebels they brought headed to the execution room. When they arrived at the throne room, they found a centaur standing over the ruins, facing the other way. He was pulling something out of the ground.

"Halt!" Thomas shouted, but the centaur did not halt. Instead, the centaur pulled Klokar's axe out of the ruins. Thomas saw this and thought that the axe might make the centaur the King of centaurs now. In any case, Thomas didn't think it mattered since the siege party wiped out most of the centaurs. "I said halt!" Thomas shouted again.

Soon everyone in the room was fighting the centaur. It was Joseph, Thomas, Bill, and fifteen Edhormond against one centaur. It seemed simple, right? Nope. Possessing the axe made the centaur as skilled in a fight as mighty Klokar.

"Die!" the centaur yelled, jumping five feet into the air and landing on Thomas. He readied to decapitate Thomas with the axe. An Edhormond blocked the strike with a spear, but died when the centaur spun around and decapitated him. Seizing this opportunity, the other Edhormond, Joseph, and Bill all jumped onto the centaur. The centaur shook them off with a single movement and used his axe to kill more Edhormond. Now only seven Edhormond remained, in addition to the rebel overseers.

"I owe my life to that dead guy over there," Thomas remarked.

"Well, he's dead. He can't hear that compliment, and it is distracting the living people here trying to stay alive. So, shut up and fight," Bill snapped.

The Edhormond charged the centaur again and two more died to the axe. The centaur turned his eyes on Thomas again. "You...will...die!" the centaur screamed. The centaur charged into Thomas, using the spike on the top of the axe haft to impale Thomas in the stomach.

"No!" Bill yelled as he pulled an arrow and shot at the centaur, landing a hit. The centaur charged Bill and Bill started frantically shooting arrows. The first two arrows missed. The third, however, was another hit and enough to finish off the centaur. For good measure, the remaining Edhormond impaled him a few times and threw his body over the throne room balcony railing. The body landed on a sharp rock, ending the battle. The Edhormond burned Klokar's axe so another centaur could never again use it. The rebels conducted a funeral for Thomas and buried him in their burial room.

Joseph could not believe the Edhormond destroyed the evil centaur race. The time was right to go after Sorwond! First, however, Joseph wanted to know more about these soldiers that just destroyed Klokar and the centaurs. "I want to know who leads the Edhormond, and where that leader is," Joseph announced in a meeting with the entire Rebellion of Broken Chains. No one knew the answer to either of those questions. "Does anyone have a clue that could help lead us to the answer?"

One soldier spoke. "I noticed the Edhormond traveling. I think they traveled southwest after leaving Klokar's palace."

Joseph knew what to do next. "If the Edhormond fail to return, we will travel southwest and investigate. If they return, we will ask them where they were."

Back at Mount Edhormon, the Edhrine met again with his second-in-command. "So, how did the final siege go?" the Edhrine asked.

"Very well. I followed the rebels and our forces in secret. No one knew I was watching."

The Edhrine was pleased. "So, is Klokar dead, and the centaurs extinct?" he asked and received confirmation from the second-in-command. "Good. After the stunt they pulled off twenty years ago with the siege party, they needed to be eliminated." The Edhrine continued, "I appoint you the Edhrine's Eye. You are skilled at watching in stealth. You will keep your status of second-in-command."

"The rebels want to know who leads us. They want to find you," the Eye told the Edhrine.

"Why is that?"

The Eye replied, "I must assume it is out of curiosity. They are not the type to respect anonymity. They want to know who leads their allies before partnering with them."

"I am fine with them knowing of my presence, so long as they take the oath of silence. The labyrinth will test them. Those who will break the oath will become lost, and those that will keep it will make it through. My sorcery lies upon the labyrinth.

It is the only way from the gates to the fortress other than the hidden passage." The Edhrine instructed the Eye to make the rebels journey as difficult as possible. He wanted to strengthen the rebels' will to honor the oath of silence and be welcomed into the gates of Edhormon.

When the Edhormond returned, Joseph asked some spearmen, "Who leads you? Can we meet your leader?"

The Edhormond told Joseph that he and the other rebels will need to take the oath of silence. "He who does not keep his oath will be forever lost in the labyrinth. He will pay for his broken trust with his life, as no food or drink shall come to he who breaks his oath." Joseph questioned the secrecy and the Edhormond replied, "It is the will of the Edhrine." Joseph agreed to the secrecy because he wanted to learn more about those who just destroyed Klokar and the centaurs. However, he silently pledged to himself to try to bend the oath if he could.

Joseph began assembling the rebels for the journey south-west to meet the leader of Edhormond. Several Edhormond approached Joseph and told the rebels to stop. The Edhormond explained to Joseph that the Edhrine had given them orders to stop the rebels. They relayed the message from the Edhrine. "Any attempts to enter the labyrinth can and will be destroyed." Joseph knew the rebellion could not storm Sorwond without the Edhormond. Therefore, he heeded the orders and waited...waited to meet the Edhrine and waited for the opportunity to gain more soldiers to attack Sorwond.

5

The Siege of Sorwond

A year had passed and the size of Joseph's army increased. Seven hundred and fifty-one soldiers were assembled in front of the old fort. Time had already begun to take its toll on the place. Wild spiders filled the old mine and its walls collapsed by raiders. The chests were thrown open, doors knocked down, and the place was in ruin. Yet, it was the starting place of the Rebellion of Broken Chains.

"Here, at this place where we started, we rally. From here, we will march out to the border of these woods. We will let loose our arrows, crush the outer guards of Sorwond, and show them we are a force to be reckoned with," Joseph declared. The rebels cheered. "But we cannot do this without much training, as they outnumber us. We must train hard and perfect our arrows. We need strong armor and weaponry. Get to work! Blacksmiths, get to the forge! Archers, get to the range! Woodworkers, get to the workshop! Lumberjacks, get to the woods! Miners, get to the caves!"

After much hard work, the Rebellion of Broken Chains was ready. The rebels made the best of everything and gained even more men. Eight hundred and thirty-four soldiers were now gathered near the old fort for counting. However, the large number came with a disadvantage. The Sorwondian King Salo knew about them. Additional Sorwondian border control guards patrolled near the border of the Centaur Woods. Rebel archers took them down, but more came to take the place of the fallen. Soon, an archer battle ensued. The rebels had two key advantages in this fight. The rebels were better equipped and trained, and they had the concealment of the woods. Conversely, Sorwondians had a much larger number of archers in reserve. The fight raged on, with dead Sorwondians piling up. Arrows flew from both sides all along the border. This battle could not go on forever, though. The rebels were not invincible and some died each day. If this continued, no rebels would remain.

"We need someone with heavy armor to go in there and get those enemy archers out of here! Any ideas?" Joseph asked the rebel leaders.

Bill answered, "We need some type of berserker with heavy armor to shatter their ranks. Perhaps he wears the heaviest armor we have, carries a heavy mace, and runs out there to crush them with that mace."

"Heavy armor still has weak points. Archers can exploit many of those gaps. What about sending lightly armored soldiers with shields and spears? They can form a shield wall to get past our Sorwondian friends," Joseph proposed instead.

Bill agreed, "Seems like a good idea, as long as they drop their shields and spears once they get close enough to slash with a sword. The spears will keep enemies away from the shield wall until they pull their swords."

Now, it was time for the rebels to ready for combat. Some of them had experience from fighting the centaurs, so to build their confidence, Joseph told them, "This is just another battle against the centaurs. Just imagine that. The difference is that these guys are not mounted on horses, so they are less of a threat to infantry. Get a wall up, shove your spears in between the shields, and keep those enemies away from the wall. Once you are close enough, drop your shield and spear, pull out your sword, and stab 'em dead!" The troops cheered and formed a formidable shield wall on the west border of Centaur Woods. The wall was a success. The rebels slew the enemy archers and enabled the rebel archers to advance. Now they had to start a siege on Sorwond, but they would need Edhormond help to complete their goal.

"Lord Salo, we have had complications on our defensive line," a militia messenger reported to the King of Sorwond. "The enemy advanced with a shield wall, and we did not have our own to combat it. They charged our archers and slew most of them. The only large force of archers left is the force of men on the walls."

Salo did not receive this report well. "I want the survivors executed. They belong to a legion that ran in cowardice from an enemy."

"Don't you think that will be too harsh? Shield walls are known for their effectiveness against archers. There is a fine line between wisely retreating from a fight you cannot win and foolishly running from one you can. I feel they were on the wise side," the messenger explained.

"I have added you to the list of death row prisoners," Salo announced. The messenger screamed in fear and disbelief as two spearmen disarmed him and dragged him to prison.

At the battlefront, the rebel shield wall was holding up, and an Edhormond messenger came to meet with Joseph. The Edhormond agreed to send two-thousand, five-hundred Edhormond spearmen and two-hundred fifty Edhormond archers to aid Joseph. The archers carried bows of black steel with yellow mist strings. Their arrows were constructed of black steel shafts fitted with yellow mist arrowheads and fletching. Rebels built three trebuchets, which were catapults used for hurling heavy stones, while crews trained to operate them and a huge battering ram. Fifty massive Edhormond berserkers would also be in the siege.

On the day of the siege, Edhormond soldiers went to Centaur Woods along with a delegation to discuss the terms of reinforcement. They agreed on a settlement that dictated all survivors of the battle from the Edhormond army would return to Edhormond, but Joseph could request them back if the need should ever arise. The army was designated the Edhormond-Broken Chain Pact Army (EBCPA), and both the Edhormond and the rebels added soldiers to the EBCPA. The EBCPA formed a shield wall and marched under Joseph's command toward Sorwond.

Once the EBCPA reached the walls of Sorwond, Sorwond's wall guards were prepared to resist their attack. The guards possessed javelins in their hands, with bows and quivers of arrows on their backs. The Edhormond soldiers put their shields above their heads, except for the front line, who put shields in front of them in the form of a shield wall. This made the only vulnerable targets the rebel spearmen, the Edhormond berserkers (who probably would just pull the javelins out of them and charge the wall), and the siege engines. A rain of javelins came from the wall onto the rebel spearmen. The spearmen managed to put up their shields in time, though. An arrow rain followed, launching from behind the wall and getting stuck in the Edhormon spearmen's shields.

The siege party slowly marched forward, berserkers in the front with rebel spearmen behind them and a phalanx of Edhormond spearmen in tow. In the phalanx, the battering ram and the three trebuchets brought up the rear. Arrows continued to rain on the phalanx, until someone blew a Sorwondian signal horn causing the Sorwond guards to redirect their aim towards the rebel spearmen. The horn blew again and arrows began falling upon the berserkers.

An EBCPA battle horn sounded and the berserkers charged the wall. The EBCPA horn blew a second time and the rebel shield wall charged. Upon the third blow, the phalanx charged with the battering ram and trebuchets. With one final blow, the trebuchets hurled their payloads towards to the Sorwondian walls. When the berserkers reached with the wall, they ripped defenders from the wall with their massive cleavers. After a few hits, the defenders managed to duck and avoid the cleavers. So, the shield wall focused on the gate. The phalanx stopped and the battering ram started to advance with soldiers moving out of the way to let it pass to the front line.

A massive legion of Sorwondian pikemen advanced to protect the gate, each man with his pike forward. This made any head-on approach by the EBCPA virtually impossible. Pikemen positioned themselves in front of the wall and made sure the battering ram could not come anywhere near the gate. Rebel spearmen began to back up, but the Edhormond would not let these primitive long stakes be their downfall. The Edhormon switched to steel javelins and began throwing them. A rain of black steel missiles fell upon the pikemen, killing many and wounding many more. Those who were still able to fight were convinced that this fight was not winnable and tried to retreat.

The rebels charged and defeated those remaining at the gate. Edhormond whipped out more javelins and threw them over the wall. Screams came from behind the stone wall as archers fell to these javelins.

The battering ram proceeded forward and reached the gate. Rebels heard a commotion among the wall guards. They realized the commotion resulted from the Edhormond javelin throwers' attack on the guards. The Edhormond phalanx put away their javelins and switched back to their spears. They lined up behind the rebels and prepared to enter Sorwond. On the ram's third strike, a flaming arrow flew over the wall onto the wooden framework of a siege engine. Luckily, someone put out the fire before it caused any damage. The rebels became concerned, though, when a small rain of flaming arrows landed on and in the area around the battering ram. The battering ram swung again, hitting the gate and catching it on fire. Soon thereafter, the battering ram collapsed, as a result of being on fire from the flaming arrows, killing the operators of the battering ram and several nearby spearmen. However, the gate also burned down before Sorwondians could douse the flames with water.

The siege was working! Men rushed in through the gate and were shocked by what they saw. Citizens were lined up in rows, blocking the path of the soldiers. The citizens were chained to posts and buildings and guards with bows were ready to fire upon the rebel siege party. One of the citizens in the front was Margaret, Joseph's mother.

Salo himself emerged from the tallest tower in the kingdom and shouted from the balcony. "Do you think I would let you in to slaughter my soldiers and murder my most trusted?"

"No," Joseph replied from within the ranks of spearmen, "I do not, but I do not expect you to place innocent people in the line of battle."

"These people are my servants! They adore me and would die for me."

Being chained up in front of an enemy phalanx appeared to weaken the effect that the spell of Salo's speeches had on the citizens. Peasants cried for mercy and for the rebels to save them. Margaret struggled with her ropes and chains, and an archer cautioned her not to resist Salo. Margaret looked at Joseph and said, "I understand now." She started to say more, but was struck and killed by an archer for speaking with the rebel leader. Joseph watched as she fell. He wanted to mourn the death of his mother, but he had a war to fight now.

Joseph looked up at the keep and raged, as did many of the other EBCPA soldiers. The Edhormond charged, climbing up the wall with ropes and ladders. Most of the guards were dead and those faking it were no longer faking it. Edhormond descended into the shattered ranks of archers behind the wall and emerged behind the archers guarding the peasants. Salo was alarmed and ran back into his tower as the Edhormond finished off the archers. The rebels freed the peasants who were in the middle of the road and instructed them to free others. Soon the road was clear and the surviving peasants left for the Centaur Woods under the escort of rebel guards. The siege was not over, though. Sorwond had to be finished. The three trebuchets began hurling payloads again. Shortly after, the tallest tower collapsed, but Salo had moved from the tower to a more stable part of the keep. He was also not alone in the keep. Spearheads in windows showed that every remaining soldier in Sorwond was also in the keep. The trebuchets continuously hurled stones into the keep, and screams were heard. Salo was still alive and Sorwondian soldiers would not surrender as long as he was. The EBCPA surrounded the keep. This was Salo's last stand.

"I want the hidden weapons unleashed. Send forth the wild things to defend Sorwond!" Salo ordered one of his most trusted generals. The general walked into a dead-end hallway in the keep. He knocked a secret code and the secret door opened. The general entered and closed the passage behind him. A guard slid the deadbolt into the locked position. No one entered without Salo's permission.

"Send the spearmen against the gate. It is time for Salo to meet his end," Joseph commanded. Edhormond spearmen formed two lines, each twenty-four men long. The formation grabbed a large iron pole and rammed the gate of the keep, causing Sorwondian guards to reposition onto the walls. Javelins started falling as the Edhormond attempted to ram the gate open. It was a matter of when, not if, the besiegers would break into the keep. As they fought, some men heard a strange noise in the distance. Maybe it was nothing, or maybe it was Salo's horrific weapon. Onto the streets ran hundreds of tortured men, women, and even children carrying daggers, pitchforks, and other weapons. In their pain they charged, their minds twisted by Salo to believe any enemy of Sorwond was responsible for their suffering and must be conquered. Defenders on the wall ran into the keep, away from the hideous sight. Some of the tortured were so twisted that they even slaughtered each other.

The Edhormond spearmen made a shield wall, unaffected by this hideous sight. The Edhormond did not have feelings and could not be affected by anything morale-related. The rebels, on the other hand, started to run from the tortured crowd of peasants. Edhormond at the gate helped the rebels regain their senses and return the rebels back into battle. The shield wall kept the tortured at bay, yet the tortured felt too much emotional pain to feel the spears. They tried to jump the shield wall. If that worked, it could be over for the EBCPA.

Tortured peasants ran up the shield wall and inserted daggers and swords into necks and backs of the EBCPA, breaching the shield wall. It became an all-out melee in the streets between rebels and Edhormond and the tortured. However, the Edhormond had brought a new type of troop for this battle. The juggernauts wore the strongest of Edhormond armor. They bore somewhat respectable hammers which, relative to the juggernauts size and strength, were small. The juggernauts could kill a man simply by stepping on him. Several of them rushed into the city and crushed the tortured. They helped the spearmen who were struggling to fight without a phalanx or an effective shield wall. Spearmen were weak in all out melees like this.

Soon the tortured were defeated and rebel reinforcements arrived from the Centaur Woods, many of them rescued citizens who had no training for combat, but felt they owed the rebels their service. The besiegers that ringed the keep placed ladders against the walls of the keep. That was a mistake. The sound of slaves grunting filled the air as some parts of the keep's walls slid outward, knocking the tall ladders down and causing them to break against houses and bastions. However, some troops got into tower balconies and started fighting. Shortswords and daggers were mainly depended on for this fight. Rebels always carried some sort of dagger or shortsword with them. The Edhormond drew small daggers and began throwing them. The yellow mist blades on their weapons lit up dark cellars, which were full of stolen goods. After many long hours of close combat and just about every secret passage and spike trap uncovered, Sorwond's keep was in ruins. Trebuchets fired the whole time, and when the besiegers reached the top, they were only a few stories above the ground as the tower was nearly leveled. Salo, at last, came out of a secret room uncovered by falling debris. Besiegers surrounded him and his small delegation of guards. The battle ended and blood covered the streets. Corpses were countless as many died. Some died bravely for both sides, and some died cowering.

The EBCPA took Salo and his delegation to the plain in between Sorwond and the Centaur Woods, and tied them to the ground with stakes and poles. Edhormond berserkers and juggernauts lined up, and could step on any one of them at any time. Edhormond and rebel spearmen made a circular shield wall around the area to prevent an escape if they broke their bonds. Other men patrolled the area to watch the spearmen's backs. Inside the perimeter, more spearmen patrolled and made sure the perimeter wall stayed alert and ready. Nothing could go wrong.

First, Joseph started by asking what sorcery Salo used in his speeches.

"I use no sorcery," lied Salo at first. "I simply have loyal subjects."

"Well, how come you had to chain and threaten your 'loyal' people to get them to block our path?"

Salo confessed that he had a sorcery altar, but he said if he did not have to give its location, he would confess more. Joseph accepted the deal, and Salo confessed that the tortured were the people who he imprisoned. Joseph then had Salo and his delegation marched to the prisons. By now, many more people than Kevin filled the prisons. Traitors, spies, snoopers, enemy mercenaries, and more were there. The prison worked like a machine. When sent to labor, a ladder would bring prisoners from their pits into metal passageways with crusher traps in case a revolt started. At work, prisoners would forge weapons and prepare food. After work, they went back to the pits and climbed down the ladder. Once all prisoners were in pits, the metal passageways closed to prevent any escapes. In addition, prisoners in one pit had no way to communicate with prisoners in another pit. This made an organized jailbreak impossible. The prison functioned well and kept prisoners in their place. What made it harder to get out was that the whole prison was underground in an area south of the underground fort Joseph and his high command structure dwelt in (this fort is also the one that Joseph made after running from the Old Fort). There was only one way in and one way out, making escaping almost impossible.

Salo and his men were put in the pits the furthest away from the entrance. To escape required getting through most of the other pits to get to the entrance, and defeat the guards who had an inward-facing shield wall there. Since guards could only leave the prison with special permission, Salo couldn't just put on a uniform and walk out on an "important mission." Salo and his men had double work shifts for what they did to the Sorwondian people, and were sentenced to work in the prisons for ten years before their execution.

The rebels eventually returned to Sorwond's ruins. They established a city there, and renamed the city as New Sorwond. People celebrated for a week, and every year that followed, people would celebrate the liberation. Salo's city, surprisingly, did not become the Sorwondian capital. Instead, the capital was born in the Centaur Woods, around the Old Fort and Joseph's current, underground fort. Joseph became the first leader of New Sorwond.

6

The Four

"So, how is Joseph's New Sorwond going?" the Edhrine asked the Eye.

"Well, they are prospering economically due to the wide variety of natural resources in the Centaur woods. The Sorwondian city is slowly being deserted, though. Most people enjoy the woods more and would rather not live near the streets that a tyrant commanded for so long." The corpses had not yet been fully cleared, so it was likely you would find a fallen rebel, tortured, Edhormond, or Sorwondian in an alley or maybe on a roof. As a result, most people were gone from there, and the ruins had not been repaired much.

"So, what about the Edhrine? Are we going to try to look for his fortress or leave him be?" one of the rebels asked Joseph.

Joseph replied, "Well, he said we would know when the 'time is right,' whatever that means."

After that short conversation about the Edhrine's whereabouts, interest sparked all throughout New Sorwond about the location of the Edhrine. There was wide agreement, even by the former rebels, that the Edhormond did the most work on the battlefield during the siege. The rebels, however, supplied the catapults and the battering ram, except for the small bit of Edhormond steel used in the head of the battering ram. They also supplied the materials for the siege engines. Nonetheless, most people, soldiers, and high command officials in New Sorwond believed they owed the victory more to the Edhrine. Everyone supported a search mission to locate the Edhormond that they felt saved them.

Reports of an Edhormond steel chariot traveling through the woods arose and people began hunting for this chariot. They seemed like rumors to Joseph, but then he saw it personally, and it stopped for him. Out came an Edhormond spearman. The spearman gave Joseph three days to decide on an offer. "You may go alone to Mount Edhormon, or you may not go at all. If you go alone, you shall return in three weeks' time. The Edhrine awaits, the forges of Edhormond steel await, and the Edhormond army awaits. That is, if you accept."

Joseph immediately decided he would go. He took the three days to pack his things, select a substitute for his position in the government, and set guidelines so the substitute would not gain too much power and have the chance to abuse that power. With that, Joseph got on the bench behind the spearman, and they sped off in a southwest direction. Some strange, stone Edhormond horse pulled the chariot. A New Sorwondian soldier took note of the direction the chariot went and gave it to an officer. They were right on in terms of the direction to Edhormon.

The chariot continued to Edhormon, and arrived at a large body of water. There, the chariot boarded a massive square raft made of Edhormond steel. On top of the barge were buildings. It was not exactly a city, but rather a small town on a military barge. There were catapults on it and groups of large bows laid horizontally. These bows had rods that kept the string back. A small beam with a groove had a projectile in it. When the rods were removed, a group of arrows launched into the air. The arrows would rain on the enemy. Apparently, the Edhrine also has a sea armada and not just an army. Joseph saw five more of these barges after only a minute on the barge. These barges were traveling from Edhormon to various places and some were returning to Edhormon.

Joseph decided to look around. He noticed no sleeping quarters, no dining room, and no washrooms. He asked the spearman, who remained next to Joseph, about this. "An Edhormond needs no sleep, food, nor drink," was the simple response. "You will stay in a room that currently stores spare spears. I assume you brought something comfortable to sleep on. If not, we have cloth mats for delicate things that can serve as sleeping mats and blankets."

After two days, Joseph and the spearman departed the raft. They got onto a larger chariot, which had a second cart behind the first one. Joseph, his guide, and a spearman commander sat in the first cart on a bench behind the driver. The second cart, from what Joseph could see, was full of spearmen. They arrived at a massive mountain that had an odd, long shape. Approaching from the east, there was a bulge in the front middle, with another one farther north. The chariot drove alongside the front bulge and reached a black gate that appeared to lead into the mountain. From there, the spearman said was the underground labyrinth. "A sorcery lies upon the labyrinth, cast by the Edhrine long ago. He who enters with intent to break the oath of silence that one must swear upon meeting the Edhrine will become lost. I cannot guide you through the maze, but I can tell you that you will know if the maze will let you through or not. None who have been deemed worthy took more than a minute to figure out the way." With that, the spearman stepped aside and Joseph entered the maze. The spearman entered the fortress through a secret door only those already worthy knew about.

Joseph found his way through the maze, and ascended a staircase. At the top, ten spearmen welcomed him and the guide brought him to the Chamber of Meeting. There was a raised platform in the very back, and a large, U-shaped table. Out of a side door came an Edhormond soldier wearing much different armor. He had a long, black cape and a Y-shaped visor rather than the standard visor. There was no frontal spike on his helmet. His armor was clearly heavier, but he walked in like the armor was lighter than air. In his belt was a long, thin sword with a yellow mist blade and black steel hilt. This was no soldier. This was the Edhrine. The Edhrine had two guards flanking him, and he walked to the platform and stood atop it. Joseph sat down in a chair directly across the table from the Edhrine's platform. The Edhrine and Joseph talked about the developments in New Sorwond and some other minor economic concerns. Then, the Edhrine started telling Joseph about the Errorunsai.

"Do you know what an Errorunsin is?" the Edhrine asked.

"No," Joseph replied, perplexed.

"Let me tell you, I am an Errorunsin. There are four Errorunsai, and I am one. I know of three other than myself, and I am an enemy with one of those three. I know the Marantaur and the Mokror and hate the Ifloract. The Marantaur lives out in some distant plains, while the Ifloract lives deep in a cave system, known as the Depths of Flame. The Ifloract and his army are opposite of me on a map of the world, situated in the Mountains of the Elements. The Mokror lives on an island in the center of the Mohraight Graveyard. She commands legions of large spiders. Her island is directly southeast of here."

Joseph took some time to take it all in, and then the Edhrine continued, "I know this is a lot of new information, but it is necessary for you to know. There is also the Prophecy of the Errorunsai. It is: Four Errorunsai there are, yet one is more powerful than the other three. This One will turn from good ways, wanting more power, bringing torment, and raising an army in secret. The Three will realize in due time what horrors are coming. A great war will break, and unknown is the outcome. Known is that this war will include many entities. Known also is that whomever wins this war shall achieve power greater than any ever known."

After a previous discussion between the Four about the Prophecy, they decided the Four would meet at Edhormon because of Joseph's presence in Edhormon. Thus, they came. First entered the Marantaur, a large beast with huge muscles, towing two maces weighing five hundred-pounds each. He wore little armor, just a spiked shoulder pad, leather trousers, and a steel helmet. Red mist seeped from the eye holes. Next was the Ifloract, whom the Edhrine pulled a sword at the sight of, and legions of spears made sure the Ifloract did nothing other than what was expected. The Ifloract was a flaming soul, with a dark, obsidian helmet for a head. Flames shot out of the eye holes in his helmet. He had arms of flame and held a strange invisible cloak of fire around him closed. When he opened the cloak, sparks flew everywhere in the room and Edhormond spearmen warned him sternly to stop with the flames. Last was the Mokror. She had full black armor with a white glowing visor. She carried a long weapon in one hand and had many small daggers to be thrown from the other. Her weapon was a sword that had an axe head on the top and a large spike on the opposite end. The Mokror commanded an army of spiders, and one came with her to the meeting. An ashen soldier with a long halberd came with the Ifloract. The only one to travel alone was the Marantaur.

The meeting's main purpose was to educate Joseph. The Errorunsai wanted to partially reveal themselves to humans. During the meeting, the Four discussed who might be the One, and why certain ones hated each other. The Edhrine and the Ifloract hated each other, and the Mokror and the Marantaur hated each other, too. Apparently, it was in a second verse of the prophecy. The Edhrine and the Mokror talked, as they had never met before for an extended period. Then, all Four talked of the prophecy. They talked about who might be the One again and accused each other. They decided that the argument was useless and moved on.

The meeting was unproductive, but everyone attended because Joseph was present. The Edhrine dismissed Joseph after the three weeks were up and was the first one to see the Edhrine who did not have to take the oath of silence. Everyone else who went to Edhormon left only after taking the oath to not reveal the location or any details of the Edhrine or Edhormon.

Joseph returned to New Sorwond after his time at the Edhrine's fortress. He transformed a rabble of men with random weapons into gleaming rank and file soldiers with issued weapons. He decided to make the heads of the polearms (spears, pikes, etc.) a rotated square shape, rather than a more common rhombus-shaped, leaf-shaped, or triangle-shaped. This soon became the symbol of New Sorwondian military forces.

Open travel between New Sorwond and Edhormon com-
menced and Edhormon constructed a little town controlled by
the Edhrine. The Edhrine was getting to know humans. The
Ifloract did similar things with nearby people. Because the
Marantaur already interacted with the tribes around him, he did
not get more involved with humans. Because no people lived
near the Mokror, and she preferred to meet with people when
she wanted and only when she wanted, she also didn't get more
involved with humans.

Joseph and the Edhrine often invited each other to their
nations to discuss the Prophecy and the growing unrest between
the Errorunsai. During one of their meetings, they discussed
how a fifth entity could bring the Errorunsai closer and better
prepare them to defend against the One. A fifth entity could also
help identify the One before the war started. The Edhrine told
Joseph that he would make a good fifth entity. The Errorunsai
knew him well enough to not kill him on sight, and he could
try to get them to drop their dislikes of each other. As much
as the Edhrine disliked the Ifloract, he knew this hate would
get in the way should they end up allied against the One. The
only downside for Joseph was that he would have to leave New
Sorwond. He could not rule New Sorwond and meet with the
Errorunsai. After thinking about the Edhrine's proposal, Joseph
agreed. He took a week to pack his things, select a replacement
leader, and build a wagon for his quarters. The wagon could
float after disconnecting the horses and wheels, so he could
also use it as a covered raft. Joseph set off on his wagon, leaving
New Sorwond behind.

7

Mohraight, Morhor, and Mountains

The Edhrine instructed Joseph to first go to the Mokror's island. He gave directions and sent Joseph off, marking the beginning of Joseph's journey. The Edhrine warned Joseph of the horrible sightings that he would encounter along the way, but nothing prepared Joseph for the rotting bodies and ships in the Mohraight Graveyard within a huge area of rocks surrounding the Mokror's home.

He saw many of the Mokror's spiders and people laying down in the grass in the distance. As Joseph approached, he saw there were rotten corpses removed, somehow, from the Mohraight Graveyard and spiders crawling all over them, taking a bite here and there. When he reached the entry to the Mokror's sewers, spiders kept the gate locked and prepared to fight. Joseph pulled out a small Edhormond steel dagger the Edhrine had once given to him. Realizing who sent Joseph, the spiders backed down.

From the tunnels came the Mokror, who opened the gate. "Did my guards give you any problems? Sorry about that."

Joseph entered and spiders led him to an empty room. It was an old prison cell with the door knocked off. There was a mat on the floor and a desk with no seat. Well, they did keep the worst criminals in sewers, and this place was a ruined sewer.

Joseph slept little during the first night. He heard noises from every direction and saw opened spider egg sacks everywhere. He used one of his shortswords to push them to a corner of the room. Luckily, these spiders were more intelligent than most, and they knew webs in the sewers would catch little. This meant that the only spider webs in the room lined the window overlooking the hallway, where insects might traverse. Joseph examined the webs, and determined the web's owner would have a feast when he came for it. After tidying his sleeping quarters, he got a few hours of sleep.

Upon waking, Joseph went to the Mokror's room. Expecting a nice room clear of webs and egg sacks, Joseph was surprised the room that webs covered the walls and egg sacks littered the floor. It was a disgusting sight. Joseph talked with the Mokror about the Marantaur. The Mokror hated the Marantaur and Joseph explained the reason for talking of her enemy. "If you end up fighting alongside the Marantaur, it would help to not hate him." The Mokror reluctantly agreed over the course of a few weeks. Joseph explained not to try anything until after he had spoken with the Marantaur to prevent the Marantaur hating the Mokror more.

After leaving Mokror's island, Joseph traveled back through the Mohraight Graveyard and into the familiar river between Edhormon and New Sorwond, which he discovered was named the Mohraight River. Joseph stopped by New Sorwond, where things were going very well. He stayed for a night and set off east toward the North Morhor Plain and the Marantaur. When he reached one tribal village, the villagers allowed him to stay at their gate for a night in his wagon. He traded a few unneeded items with the people and then went to his wagon for some sleep.

A ringing bell unexpectedly awoke Joseph. He got up, grabbed his shortswords, and looked outside. Villagers from another village charged into view. He looked backwards and saw the town ready to respond with archers and javelins. Joseph stayed neutral in the fight, and made his neutrality clear by keeping his swords in their sheaths and not moving much. During the fight, the raiders started chanting the name of Joseph's next objective. "Marantaur! Marantaur! Marantaur!"

The Marantaur came running in out of nowhere. Defenders fled in fear from the two great maces of the Marantaur. Archery fire was now the key to bringing the attack down, which would get an Errorunsai out of the picture. However, Joseph doubted the Marantaur would go down that easily. Arrows fell in large numbers, sinking into the Errorunsin's flesh. Would he go down? No. Joseph watched him take the hits like flies landing on him. Soon the two great maces were falling upon the steel barred gate. It burst open and raiders entered, while the Marantaur remained outside to pull out the arrows.

At this time Joseph approached the Marantaur. "I am he who is sent by the Edhrine, as you may have heard."

The Marantaur grumbled. "Why are you interrupting me? Have you not learned not to interrupt someone recovering from a battle?"

Joseph took his wagon to the Marantaur's home village. The villagers told him to park inside, but Joseph insisted on parking outside. Joseph talked with the Marantaur and they discussed the Mokror. After a week of discussion, the Marantaur still would not budge his opinion of the Mokror. Joseph tried for another week, and the Marantaur grew angry just hearing the Mokror's name. Another week, and more openly hostile reactions came. The Marantaur would raise a mace sometimes, but usually calmed down. Joseph also noticed the Marantaur did not want Joseph gone from the village. The Errorunsin would hang out by the gate at night. One night, Joseph snuck over the wall and reached his wagon and left in the night. Joseph's next trip would be the hardest one. He was going to the Ifloract. This was he who hated the Edhrine, and he whom the Edhrine hated.

Joseph traveled through the South Morhor Mountains and saw the Mountains of the Elements in the distance. He knew there was sorcery there for all of the elements, and the sorcery dominated the areas. The areas were: Ravine of Air, Valley of Earth, Peak of Frost, and Depths of Flame. The Ifloract dwelt within the Depths of Flame. Joseph knew the legions of guards would kill him at a moment's notice, as one sent by the Edhrine. Joseph removed the Edhormond flag on his wagon and put it in a cabinet in his small cooking space. If the ashen soldiers demanded a search, he was dead meat. Because the town where humans interacted with the Ifloract's forces was in the South Morhor Mountains, the guards had every reason to be suspicious of him, and nobody was there to call Joseph's death wrong. Joseph could not be caught. After removing the Edhrine's flag, he displayed a white flag, so he could show he was not coming in hostility. He put his weapons in a small case so guards would not know that he was armed. He could rip them out if needed. Joseph continued down the hill to the Depths of Flame's entrance. A legion of soldiers in a phalanx blocked his path. The soldier's halberds were very long, longer than most New Sorwondian pikes. The halberds were held two-handed or one hand with the sharp rear end in the ground. Joseph knew these axe and spear heads could be used against him at any moment, and Joseph hid his wagon in some nearby bushes and trees. He came, weapons hidden, holding a white flag small enough not to draw attention but big enough where his good intentions were clear. He started walking alongside the formation wearing a hood, and most of the soldiers failed to react to him since they faced inward and only saw a hooded figure with a white flag.

Two soldiers walked up to Joseph and lowered their halberds to face toward Joseph. "Why are you here?" they asked.

Joseph replied, "I wish to see the Ifloract. I need to speak with him in person."

The soldiers led him into the passage. He was in, but he had halberds at attack range on his neck. The guards led Joseph in deeper, and the heat grew more intense. Once the party got to the deepest level, the soldiers ordered Joseph to stay put. Joseph was thousands of yards below the top of the volcano that was atop the Depths of Fire. Further below was a large pool of magma. If this was a volcano, he hoped it would not erupt any time soon. The soldiers looked into the magma and bowed, warned Joseph that snooping around would be costly, and left.

After several minutes of waiting, the lava at the bottom started to bubble and rise. Joseph became uneasy. Then, it rose in a tube shape and splashed back into the pool, and the Ifloract stood before Joseph. The Ifloract was basically an obsidian helmet atop a great flame. The Ifloract's flame was intense, and a fiery cloak kept it from spilling out and burning everything in its path. "What do you seek?" the Ifloract asked.

Joseph replied, "I seek your hospitality. I have, so far, been with three of the four Errorunsai, and you are the last I have visited. Although this may not be to your pleasure, I was sent by the Edhrine."

"Why do I owe one sent by my enemy my hospitality? Why do I have to allow what could easily be a saboteur past my lines?" The Ifloract seemed to be asking himself now. "Why do I not owe you my wrath?" His flame cloak opened, and fire and magma spewed out in all directions. Joseph took cover behind a rock, and some living flames entered with ashen soldiers. They realized what was going on and exited as quickly as possible. "Fine," decided the Ifloract. He pulled closed the invisible cloak of flame with fiery hands. The hands once again melted in with the rest of the Ifloract's flame. "You can stay, and do what you must. You are not the Edhrine. You did not wrong me. Now go to your place before I change my mind. Soldiers, show him to his room." With that, the Ifloract descended into the pool of magma and disappeared.

Four living flames escorted Joseph to his room. Midway, Joseph pointed out that his belongings were in his wagon. The flames escorted him up top, Joseph got what he needed, and went back down with them to his room. It was on the bottom floor, which was good because he could walk right over to the Ifloract's magma pool, but bad because the heat was at its hottest temperature. Joseph put down his sleeping mat, but realized it would make him too hot, so he decided to sleep on the rock floor. He used his shortswords to smooth out the ground, so he would not injure himself on rocks during the night.

For the next few weeks, Joseph explained his intentions for bringing the Errorunsai closer. The Ifloract remarked, "The Edhrine was wise to say that, but the sting of one of the four betraying will make one mad. One Errorunsin can join the One who betrayed in his madness, and the Errorunsai could fall this way."

Joseph felt differently. "The sting will give them a greater need for revenge, and they can harness this and hit the One hard."

They discussed this, and decided the Errorunsai were strong-headed people, considering how long they lived and battled for centuries. The Ifloract eventually agreed with Joseph, and the Ifloract decided he would partner with the Edhrine.

8

The Beginning

Joseph returned to Edhormon, where the Edhrine agreed to build Joseph a room. Unlike most rooms, Joseph's room was located in the labyrinth. The Edhormond simply made a large room for Joseph's wagon with a comfortable bed and desk, as an alternative to the cramped wagon. The Edhrine promised to have soldiers clean the room regularly, so it did not end up like the Mokror's place. The Edhrine also gave him a partner. This Edhormond was stronger than most, and would assist Joseph in his travels. He could row fast and help move heavy loads.

The Edhrine and Joseph discussed the Marantaur's aggressive reaction to Joseph's attempt to bring him closer to the Mokror. "It is suspicious indeed," said the Edhrine, "but we cannot judge him based on one test. I have a second one in mind, and you will have to go to the others again. There is reason why I did not wish for you to do both tests at once. This does not involve the relationship between the Errorunsai, but the Marantaur may not take kindly to your arrival."

"There is one slight problem about going back to the Marantaur," Joseph noted and explained how he fled the village.

"I will arrange a meeting with the Marantaur to be sure nothing uneasy exists between you and the Marantaur,"

"That would be good. Thank you."

The Edhrine went outside and through the guarded entrance to the upper part of the fortress. Joseph and his new assistant readied everything for departure the following morning. Joseph got some sleep while the assistant simply stood guard because there was nothing else for him to do. In the morning, they both got in the wagon. The assistant volunteered to steer, and Joseph sat in the back cooking. Joseph cooking his food was more efficient than trading for food, and Joseph was a surprisingly good cook. They arrived at the Mokror's first and executed the second test.

"What do you think the best way to prepare for the One would be?" Joseph asked.

"Well, I feel sheer strength of arms will not do. Forging a better relationship with each other is key. I will start trying with the Marantaur," answered the Mokror.

Joseph told the Mokror about his time with the Marantaur, and the Mokror felt it was important to try to strengthen the relationship, but agreed it would be risky considering the Marantaur's temper. Joseph and his assistant stayed and planned with the Mokror for each Errorunsin being the One, aside from the Mokror herself.

Next, Joseph went to the Ifloract, who responded to the test question differently. "Raising strong my legions is important, but crucial to victory is for the Errorunsai to have a strong base and relationship with nearby people. If the people side with you, they will unite under the banner of the Three. Their involvement or disinterest will create or destroy our chances of victory."

After the Ifloract, was the Marantaur. The Marantaur welcomed Joseph in slightly uneasily, and responded to the question in a very different manner. "He who bears the greatest armament will see victory, whether he is the One or one of the Three. Build strength in legions as far as the eye could see, and drill soldiers not much short of all day and in their free time train more."

Joseph's stay with the Marantaur was brief because of the uneasiness between them. Upon returning to Edhormond, Joseph learned of unsettling news. Just after he left the Marantaur, the Marantaur destroyed the village he was in. He left, smashing buildings down on his way out. Nobody has seen or heard from him since.

Upon hearing the news, Joseph said, "He is the One. He knew we were eying him. He knew. He bailed out before legions from across the lands stormed him. He responded with strength of arms, although he does not have an army at all. It doesn't add up."

"He is the One," the Edhrine also concluded. "Tell the Ifloract and the Mokror to come for a meeting, and make sure they put heavy guard before their departure."

The Prophecy was fulfilled sooner than expected.

The Three and Joseph met at Edhormon. They decided full military action was required. The Mohraight Graveyard was covered in spiders. Edhormond returned to the New Sorwond area and the Centaur Woods. Soldiers from the Depths of Flame marched through the South Morhor Mountains. Everything except for the barbaric reaches of the northeast regions was ready for anything. In the meeting, the Edhrine and Ifloract quickly set aside their differences. Joseph's work in his first round of traveling paid off.

The Ifloract announced, "In the South Morhor Mountains,

I saw several armed men. They did not have a uniform, and resembled the original army that conquered Sorwond City."

The Mokror replied, "I attained information from New Sorwondians about similar men in the North Morhor Plain. I don't like this. It seems the Marantaur may be raising an army in secret."

The Edhrine responded, "We must take action. New Sorwond can help greatly. We need to find other civilizations that can help us, too."

"I will go look south," volunteered Joseph.

"No, it is too risky, Joseph," replied the Edhrine. Everyone nodded their agreement. The meeting concluded with a determination of the need for military strength and alliance with New Sorwond's new leader.

Joseph still saw the need to travel south to search for possible allies. During the night, he and his assistant packed their wagon with everything they needed and went to shore. Most of the Edhormond were in the fortress, so it was easy to get to the Mohraight Graveyard. From there, they sailed south and exited the Mohraight Graveyard. Joseph had gotten used to the corpses by now, so it was an easy trip through the graveyard. They did not get far before they encountered great fleets of ships bearing a banner with an upside-down pitchfork sailing around, patrolling. Joseph reached a fork in the Mohraight River. If they went left, cities lined both sides of the river. Going right, cities lined only one side of the river. They went left and Joseph heard the sounds of battle. He saw ships from the upside-down pitchfork nation and from a nation that had a cross on its flag, with a circle over the middle of the cross. Four swords projected out of the circle towards the corners, and two spears were in the circle. He heard a cry from the cross ships, "For

Nacreato!" screamed some sailors. So, that side was Nacreato. "For Mohraight!" came sailors on the ships with the upside-down pitchfork flags. Joseph now knew that at least two nations were here. That was good enough. The war would affect them, and when it did, the Three might get at least two allies. That is, if they could set aside their differences to fight against the One rather than each other.

After a week of sailing, Joseph returned to Edhormon. The Edhrine did not mind that Joseph fled during the night, but he warned Joseph not to try that again because he was needed alive. Joseph learned of more disturbing news. His replacement leader in New Sorwond did not accept the Three's alliance proposal. Joseph agreed to go to New Sorwond to see if he could do anything, but after getting some rest. Additionally, the New Sorwondian leader wouldn't allow Edhormond soldiers into the nation. That made the first line of defense right in front of Edhormon. They needed to move their first line further west for this war to be successful. They also needed safe passage through New Sorwond to strike the One's inner territory.

After getting some rest, Joseph traveled to New Sorwond. When he arrived, he noticed things had changed. There was a wall around the outside, and the New Sorwondian flag hung from every tower and bastion. He was let in through a gate, and the town greeted him with crowds and cheers. He went to the capital, escorted to the leader by New Sorwondian officials. They discussed the matter, and New Sorwond agreed to resist the Marantaur. Initially, they believed that staying out of the battle would keep them safe, but they realized the risks they would be taking with that approach. The risk of ambush, con-quer, or takeover by influence would be high. New Sorwondians set up guard on their eastern flank and the square pike and spear heads protruded out of walls, bastions, towers, and shield walls. Archers lined up, ready to rain arrows, and Edhormond spearmen marched in. Joseph went back to Edhormon, his goal completed.

When Joseph returned to Edhormon, the Three greeted him and requested for him to lead an expedition into the North Morhor Plain to evacuate any tribes who wanted to escape the danger zone. Joseph suggested that the Three make a flag, which they did. The flag had numbers in Edhormond runes.

"The one in the middle means three, and it is there for obvious reasons," the Edhrine explained. "The runes at the top right corner and the bottom left corner both mean one. The top right stands for New Sorwond as an ally, and the bottom left stands for you," pointing to Joseph. The Edhrine continued, "The number of people personally helping us without a nation will grow, and you will be at the head of these ranks."

9

The Refugees

After a week of rest, Joseph and a small strike force set out for the North Morhor Plain, where enemies hide among friends, and friends hide among enemies. They reached the ruins of the village Joseph visited when he came to the Marantaur for the first time. There was rising campfire smoke near one of the buildings. Joseph crept closer with the Edhormond spearmen, New Sorwondian stealth fighters, and some of the Mokror's giant spiders. Joseph directed a spider to go to the top of a building and it easily scaled the wall. The spider reported a harmless-seeming green flag hanging from the front window. The flag was the sign that these people were going to Edhormon. Joseph knocked on the door using a secret knock, and the door opened. The family packed bags and led Joseph and the strike force to a tribe that wanted to leave. Other strike teams eventually led the family to New Sorwond, where they could settle or move to the town near Edhormon. Either way, they were free from the Marantaur. At least, they were free from him until he conquered them. No. Joseph forced himself to not think that way. They would win, and everyone would be free. He freed two more tribes in the same way. Another family led him to his fourth tribe in total. The gate was shut. He heard sounds of men laughing and chains being pulled out of crates.

"The Marantaur's militia is here," mouthed Joseph. He held on to a spider to scale the wall. "What do you think you're doing?" Joseph asked as he witnessed the militia lining up citizens in chains. These soldiers very much fit the Mokror's and the Ifloract's descriptions.

"Intruders!" shouted the militia men.

They didn't get far in approaching Joseph. Spiders started bouncing around in their ranks, biting the soldiers and causing immense pain. It was very effective, but disgusting to watch. The Edhormond on the wall ran down the stairs into the village and slaughtered the raiders with ease. Joseph's side suffered no casualties except for a spider whose leg was pulled off by a spearman holding on to it. That spider's partner slipped and a single spider couldn't hold the weight of a whole spearman plus his armor. Joseph and the others continued on and liberated two more villages.

Joseph returned to Edhormond with only a spider missing a leg for a casualty. Everyone was impressed including the Edhrine. The Mokror and Ifloract suggested searching the land south of which Joseph found. In his wagon, Joseph led a group of Edhormond barges. These rafts were big, so they had to go around the Mohraight Graveyard, which took a little longer. When Joseph's floating wagon came out from the slight fog of the area around the Mohraight Graveyard, nobody responded. When the massive Edhormond rafts appeared, everyone responded. A fleet of Mohraight ships surrounded them within minutes, and they boarded the Edhormond command barge. Joseph and his assistant rowed the wagon over there and boarded, too. They talked with the Mohraight officials. When they saw Joseph, the Mohraight officials declared that the military presence was not welcome here. When the spearmen came, the officials were terrified. How could yellow mist be a spearhead? What was that black steel? These were the same questions Joseph had when he first met the Edhormond.

Joseph and some Edhormond spearmen spent several hours with the officials. Joseph explained everything from the beginning at Sorwond City to the Edhrine to New Sorwond to the Errorunsai and to the present. Nacreato and Mohraight leaders agreed to make peace with each other and together go to war against the Marantaur, once they both saw fit. For now, they kept waging war on each other. They would set aside their differences once the Marantaur made the first move. That was good enough.

While there, Joseph and his assistant learned the names of the nations in the southlands. They were: Mohraight Kingdom, Nacreato, Monfor, Laste, Traste, Acronomon, Lacon, Zser, Zygyptania, and Ysio. Aside from Mohraight and Nacreato, the nations refused any action in the war until they were affected. They constantly waged war like the tribes of the North Morhor Plain, but on a much larger and more elaborate scale. Ballistae and catapults sat atop the towers on rafts and ships like kings on high thrones. Some ballistae even fired whole bundles of bolts, resulting in a shotgun-like splash area at close range. Even some southern crossbows could do this. They called them machine ballistae and machine crossbows. Elaborate trench systems were well-constructed and defended and required trained assassins to clear. Joseph watched a Mohraight trench clearance drill and was impressed by the tactics used.

Back in Edhormon, the Edhrine met with the Eye. "Is there

anything that we should discuss?" the Edhrine asked the Eye.

"Yes, we need to discuss my use. We do not need to watch the humans in New Sorwond. What shall I do?"

"You are now under Joseph's command. He needs you more than I do, so go. Reveal to him your identity. Take not the removal of your second in command status as a slight, but rather as a blessing. You now can go with Joseph and help him command legions of militia in the making."

"By your command."

When Joseph returned, the Eye greeted him. The Eye informed Joseph that he was his new assistant, and would help with stealthily watching enemies and friends alike. He explained his previous service to the Edhrine and its end. Joseph readied a place and job in the wagon for the Eye.

10

The First Strike

With the Eye's duties settled, Joseph turned to the war effort. It was suspected that the Marantaur's army would be on the march by the next week, which did not leave a lot of time. The Edhrine told Joseph to move to the Sacred River and stay there, so he could quickly respond to action in that area. The Edhrine also gifted Joseph a new assistant, who was a soldier specially designed with superior strength. The soldier had strong arms and legs, and could row the wagon very quickly. This strength also made him effective in combat with blunt weapons like the two Edhormond steel hammers he carried. The strong Edhormond was nicknamed Anvil because some joked that he was as strong as a falling anvil. Anvil wore basic Edhormond steel armor, minus the helmet. Instead, he wore an old rebel helmet from the days before New Sorwond. The Eye started to wear a black cloak over his Edhormond steel armor. He already had a special helmet to avoid being seen, so the helmet stayed the same.

Joseph and his Edhormond assistants set off for the Sacred River, which traverses through New Sorwond. It was the same river that ran by the Old Fort. Unfortunately, Joseph wouldn't get to see the Old Fort because he would be much further south. When he arrived, he noticed Nacreato and Mohraight soldiers in defensive positions because of the bitter enemies that they were. This minimized the chance of minor skirmishes done purposefully. Hopefully, they could effectively set aside their differences if a war against the Marantaur was necessary.

A New Sorwondian watcher rang a bell. This was it. Joseph had a good view from his position of the hill the militia charged down. They bore banners having brown backgrounds and a red circle in the middle. It was a simple flag, but the origins of this militia were far more than simple. Joseph and his duo got ready for a fight. They charged out a gate in a wall and leapt into the line of charging militia. New Sorwondian pikes kept the Marantaur militia away from the wall, but one part only had spearmen. Joseph went over there with Anvil. They got behind the shield wall and projected spears from dead men out over the alive spearmen's heads. This ensured that nobody could jump the shield wall. Joseph noticed some Mohraight men pulling out machine crossbows. He instantly recognized the packs of arrows the men were pulling out as those that fired multiple arrows at once. He also noticed Nacreato men pulling out the machine crossbows behind him and getting ready to engage.

Joseph and Anvil let the Nacreato machine cross-bowers protect the spearmen, which allowed them to charge into a wooded area where they detected movement. Joseph and Anvil had placed the spears they picked up back into the hands of their fallen owners before leaving, and they pulled out their standard weapons. They found none other than the Eye in the bush stalking a group of Marantaur militia men who had two Nacreato prisoners. He silently pulled an Edhormond steel bow out of a case that was strapped to him. It had the usual yellow mist string and Edhormond steel bow limb. He pulled out Edhormond steel arrow shafts with yellow mist arrowheads and yellow mist fletching. It was a standard Edhormond bow set, but the Eye pulled it out like it was the most valuable in the world. He drew the string, concentrated, and fired at the group of enemies. He hit the leader square in the neck. He drew again, but loosened the string and did not fire. He motioned for everybody to be quiet. Behind them, a group of militia men were secretly heading north to New Sorwond's unprepared defenders. Once the men close to the bush were gone, Joseph, Anvil, and the Eye ran for their wagon and set out for New Sorwond.

As Joseph, Anvil, and the Eye rushed off to New Sorwond, the Marantaur strategized with leaders within his newly formed militia.

"How is the siege of New Sorwond going?" the Marantaur asked.

"Very, very well," responded a militia general. "Our southern attack is causing the desired distraction while our men march through the Centaur Woods towards the heart of New Sorwond. With the men garrisoned in the watchtowers already engaged in fighting, we will walk right in and steal victory. Your phase begins, Marantaur."

Joseph and his duo reached New Sorwond and warned the guards of a pending attack. New Sorwondians made a shield wall along the front and pikemen projected their long shafts over the shield wall for a longer reach. Available Nacreato and Mohraight machine ballistae were wheeled in behind the line to defend against many troops attacking from one area. They were ready. At least, they thought they were. Men burst out of the trees into the small clearing and charged toward the heart of

New Sorwond, and stopped dead in their tracks when they saw the defense. The attackers were surprised. Then, the defenders were surprised when the Marantaur came out of nowhere and charged at the pikes and shields. The machine ballistae no longer had a large concentration of enemy men as their target, but rather a large enemy Errorunsin. The defenders recovered from the shock and readied themselves. Pikemen raised their pikes and projected them towards the charging Marantaur, and machine ballistae fired bursts into the big beast. Spearmen held their shields tighter. Nothing killed the beast. The Marantaur let out a terrible scream and smashed a number of pikes with one swing of his mace. He advanced closer to the line. The militia men were doing little because they relied on the Marantaur. They followed behind him and cut a few pikes in half here and there.

Machine ballistae did the most damage to the Marantaur out of everything. If they could get a bolt through that thick, tank-like skin, they could kill the Marantaur. Joseph, Anvil, and the Eye started firing away with bows and crossbows from fallen men. They aimed for the Marantaur's helmet eye holes. They were exposed, but they moved so much from the Marantaur shaking his head in rage that a clear shot at one was nonexistent. A machine ballista tried, but the shaking was too much. He shook so much that a large burst of bolts couldn't pierce them either. Eventually, the Marantaur fell back, probably to pull all of the javelins and arrows out of him. The militia continued the fierce thrust, cutting pikes and charging into the massive hole in the pike line that the Marantaur made. They tried crawling, they tried climbing, they tried head-on charging. Nothing worked. Like their commander, they retreated.

11

Annihilation

For now, the Three had won the day. They had three allies. Even so, they decided the rune for one in the bottom left corner of the flag would remain. Only one person helped the Errorunsai, and nobody else's help could predate that of Joseph. Therefore, Joseph had a permanent symbol on the flag of the Three.

Joseph, Anvil, and the Eye went to the South Morhor Mountains to see where these militia men came from. They did not resemble the villagers of the North Morhor Plain. Those villagers' skin had a slightly darker tint and these fighters had lighter skin. Joseph glanced around and noticed a few who looked like them in the South Morhor Mountains. He also found cave entryways guarded by these militia men. Joseph took off his famous red cape and put away his two shortswords. Anvil and the Eye told him he now looked like any random person. Joseph went up to the guards, who told him to stay away from their homes. Joseph ran, pretending to be terrified. He went back and confirmed that these guys seemed to live here. He started checking the unguarded caves. Most of them were just caves, but a few had small houses in them. Houses. They weren't tents, so this was no army camp. There were women and children, too, as Joseph saw them in some of the caves. These men lived here. Joseph left before the guards spotted him. Now, he knew that the militia men were really dwellers of the South Morhor Mountains.

Joseph returned to Edhormon with this new information. The Edhrine considered it valuable. "If we strike them with gunpowder right at the heart in the South Morhor Mountains, we can shake their caves into collapse. We can go in and steamroll them, and the Marantaur will need to look for another army," said the Edhrine.

"There are civilians there, though," Joseph cautioned. "If we steamroll through with gunpowder, we will destroy not just military homes; we will kill the women and children."

The Edhrine replied, "So what do we do? Let them build up their troops for us to fight? Their lives will go for the greater good. Either their people or the people of many nations will be affected. The enemy won't be afraid to do these kinds of things to New Sorwond. We need to strike first to prevent their power from reaching peak strength. We must strike to the point that it is too risky for them to strike back."

"You make a valid point," said Joseph. "I agree that more lives are worth more than fewer, but I still can't do this one. I can't place the gunpowder myself. Maybe my duo can, but not me. I'll help them in any way I can from the wagon or by watching for guards, but I won't place a single hidden gunpowder charge."

"Okay," accepted the Edhrine, "only one problem. Before we can do this, you or someone else must accept another hard mission. You must break into a few villages and see what sort of objects they have, so we can model our charges to look like them. If something will be hard to explain, steal it. The owners will be gone in time."

Joseph and his assistants set out to the South Morhor Mountains. They searched for objects they could model. They donned the disguise of rich travelers and bribed people for their silence and objects. After accumulating enough objects, they returned home.

Next, Joseph traveled to Traste, a nation in the south. Traste agreed to help the Three, sort of. They would help with industrial needs, but they wouldn't fire any shots. Traste men got to work, and Joseph, Anvil, and the Eye got to watch it happen. Joseph felt uneasy knowing the purpose of their work. It was interesting to watch them work, though. They saw the precise replication of South Morhor vases, cups, cloths, and other items being meticulously completed. The items were first made with a part separated, and the object and its missing piece were sent to another group, where the objects were stuffed with gunpowder and sealed. Joseph made sure every charge was full and no sabotaging occurred. One charge that didn't explode meant that the entire chain reaction could fail, and surviving guards may catch up to Joseph and his group.

A few weeks later, and everybody was ready for the sabotage. Joseph made sure he was in position. When local messengers announced it was time, the sabotage mission began. Joseph stayed with the wagon. After a few hours, the men came back reporting success. They lit one of the objects at the start of the trail and sped off. A loud boom and some cracking noises were heard. They went back to inspect the damage. The caves they hit were either collapsed or empty due to the blast concussion. Surviving guards ran. Success. Joseph and his duo came back. It was difficult for Joseph to annihilate almost an entire race of people, but necessary for everybody else's survival.

Upon return, Joseph did not get a break. He had to go out to the front lines and fight hand to hand. This time the combat was in his home nation of New Sorwond. The wagon arrived to a hidden area. Once there, Joseph and his men got into disguises. The enemy could not know of Joseph's presence, and they could not know about the army of Nacreato skirmishers hiding all over the city that arrived earlier. New Sorwondian officials moved some Nacreato skirmishers, disguised as criminals being marched in for trial, into the New Sorwondian Governmental Saferoom (NSGS), which was the new name for the underground fort that Joseph made after the discovery of the Old Fort. The location of the NSGS was hardly secret anymore. Citizens went there for many reasons and a road led up to the cave. The skirmishers hid in the rooms that stored valuables, while Joseph hid in the head overseer's office with two elite Nacreato skirmishers. This office used to be Joseph's. It looked almost identical, aside from some extra items on the desk.

The following morning, enemy soldiers marched into New Sorwond. Citizens hid in homes while militia marched through the streets and tore down New Sorwondian flags and replaced them with their own flag. New Sorwondian officials planned to strike the enemy when they attempted to loot the buildings. The militia also commandeered the Centaur Woods. South Morhor men were in the streets and in the woods, but would they make that fatal mistake of searching a cave or a building? The New Sorwondian plan counted on it and the enemy did make that fatal mistake. Commanders ordered groups of men to search a house or two or check out a cave for any New Sorwondians. Skirmishers killed any militia men who entered their rooms or buildings. In the bigger buildings, it was safe in the halls, but not in the rooms.

Joseph remained waiting in the NSGS. Soon an important-looking militia man came with two spearmen in front of him. They all had things that could work as spears and shields, but no two spearmen were equipped alike in this militia. When they entered the door, a shield wall protected the important-looking guy. Once the group entered the room, the skirmishers and Joseph leapt up behind the group and killed the spearmen. The leader surrendered. Joseph peeked into the hallway. Clear. He went to the old prison, which was now used as a holding cell. There were some skirmishers in there, waiting. The skirmishers gagged the prisoners in the small cellblock to prevent them from alerting the militia. Joseph shoved the militia leader into the room. The skirmishers gagged him, too, and threw him in a cell. The noise attracted attention. Some militia came in and fell almost instantly. Joseph snuck back to the head overseer's office with his two skirmishers. When the day ended, the enemy numbers in New Sorwond were a quarter of what they were before. Militia men were uneasy with this hidden killer somewhere in their ranks. Well, it wasn't in their ranks but it seemed so to the militia men.

The plan called for the skirmishers to change tactics and begin charging. Messengers disguised as civilians entered the various houses and told the skirmishers that once men were in the streets, they were to join. The few that went first listened for various signals. In Klokar's palace, it was the alarm bell. In the woods, it was war cries. In the capital, it was feet stomping to sound like a phalanx of New Sorwondian soldiers coming. Joseph and the skirmishers in the NSGS positioned themselves next to the secret-not-so-secret door. They heard what sounded like the non-sharp end of spears being thrust into the ground. It was the feet stomping. Joseph and his men removed their disguises, went out, and ran down the short path to the capital city. They found skirmishers everywhere, throwing daggers, axes, and even spears. There was melee fighting and sleight-of-hand surprise dagger throws. It was intense, but it was also easy. The few hundred skirmishers in the city outnumbered what was left of the enemy militia.

12

The Battle Rages

Joseph returned to Edhormon, where there was some excitement. The Edhormond had made crossbows using their black steel. Crossbows were unusual and awkward for Edhormond soldiers. Even with training, using a crossbow made little sense to the Edhormond. With other weapons, using them came naturally. So, the crossbows were handed off to Joseph with string drawstrings so a non-Edhormond could use them because when a non-Edhormond uses an Edhormond weapon with yellow mist, the yellow mist disappears. Joseph practiced. TWANG! It was somewhat loud when he held it right next to his head. He lowered it a little. Twang! Joseph grew tired pulling the drawstring. He had to use the small pedal on the crossbow prod, and the crossbow would stand straight up, aiming down. If Joseph's foot stayed on the pedal, though, the crossbow didn't tip over in any direction. He bent down and grabbed the string and tried to stand up straight again, using his back and arms to pull the string. Even so, it was exhausting. He tried adding a spring of sorts, but it made the crossbow fire a shorter distance. Next, he tried making the spring removable. It was difficult,

73

but worked. However, it took more time to fire and it didn't fire much farther. He did want to make this a machine crossbow, though.

Joseph decided to go to Nacreato to learn about machine crossbows. The Edhrine permitted and he went. While there, he learned much about Nacreato. They had some food that Joseph enjoyed, and the nation was mostly desert with a little bit of forest on the eastern end. Joseph learned how to make machine crossbows and how they needed wider butts and beams. Joseph made a crossbow-bolt bundle, which was the ammunition for machine crossbows. He fired his newly made machine crossbow at long range. It had decent range, and the bolts all reached target distance. The only problem was that you could not aim specific, single shots. Therefore, he made big bolts, which took up the same amount of space as the bundle, but fired accurately and one at a time. He could now snipe and spray with a single crossbow. He went off to start teaching New Sorwondians how to make what he called semi-machine crossbows.

With Joseph's new semi-machine crossbow constructed, he returned to Edhormon for a war update. War was now raging by the Ifloract's territory. The remaining men of Marantaur's militia were there, but Joseph did not see this as a wise military tactic. It was a risky thrust to do with your last troops, unless these weren't the last troops. Maybe the Marantaur reserved a population of mountain men in the North Morhor Plain. Either way, Joseph had to help fend off the attempted invasion. He went to the Ifloract and once there spoke with him. The Ifloract told Joseph, "I have more enemies than the Marantaur right now. I am not the only elemental here. There are others, though not as physical as me. They are, for example, a large tree in the Valley of Earth to command the tree-like ents, or a misty pit in the Ravine of Air to control the great storms that are few in number yet extremely powerful. Also, there is the greatest enemy to me of all the elementals: The great ice sculpture of a king on a throne that commands legions of icy spears from atop the Peak of Frost. Ice is my natural enemy. We are all aware that ice and fire naturally struggle, and that holds true here. Now, I won't vanquish them because there is no point. I could lift a finger and vanquish any of them, but I don't. I let them fight the stalemate, and only defend myself. It takes legions to defend, and we need legions to defend instead against the siege of the militia. Hopefully my elemental enemies attack from the same flank, which I doubt. These guys love to outflank."

Militia men approached from the north, so the Ifloract prepared his troops for an attack from the north, south, and west. To the east was the volcano that sat atop the Depths of Flame and acted as a natural defense barrier. The militia men's numbers were not small, but were dwarfed by the Ifloract's troops. It was a respectable siege party, yet this army was the only one, at least, that's what everybody thought. With the Marantaur for a commander, stupid thrusts were possible. As the militia charged, ents from the forests ran up from the south alongside icy statues of spearmen. From the west came a great storm. The Ifloract was surrounded. Although superior to each of these forces, their concurrent attack would be a struggle for the Ifloract.

They heard marching feet approaching from the west, behind the great storm. It was the Edhrine. Legions of Edhormond came and at the front stood the Edhrine, holding his longsword forward. From the north, behind the militia, came countless spiders. Once most of the arachnids advanced into view, the Mokror was visible atop a cliff that spiders climbed down like a river. The rivers of black, furry arachnids made a lake at the bottom, and the lake moved in behind the militia. Six spiders carried the Mokror, and she began charging with her lake of spiders. However, the Three's trap did not go as expected. The Edhormond threw spears and fired arrows into the great storm, yet it raged on. Weakened by the spears and arrows, the storm swallowed the Edhormond attack like a frog does to flies. The Ifloract's legions moved to the great storm and helped conquer it, and the Edhormond moved into the inner circle. Next, they focused their efforts to defeat the ents, icy spearmen, and the remaining militia.

From the west came the rumbling of footsteps, and over the horizon came the Marantaur. The Edhormond made a shield wall in combination with the Ifloract's long halberds projecting out. They readied for the Marantaur's arrival. CLASH! The Marantaur's maces swept halberds to the side and out of the way. He ripped through the shields of the Edhormond like a weight through wet paper. More halberds tried to hinder the Marantaur, but with maces swinging through the air, he subdued them all. Joseph, Anvil, and the Eye were sitting next to the entryway to the Depths of Fire when the Marantaur began running. The three immediately pulled out ranged weapons. Joseph fired bursts with his semi-machine crossbow, also firing the occasional single shot. Anvil and the Eye got out an Edhormond bow and the Eye took a few shots as Anvil watched idly.

Eventually, the militia men fell and the Errorunsai regrouped the diminished ranks of soldiers fighting the Marantaur. It was chaos. The Three, Joseph, and his two assistants prepared to fight the Marantaur hand to hand. Ranks of soldiers were soon gone, and a melee followed. The Three discovered that organized phalanx, shield wall, and formation did not work against the Marantaur. They required North Morhor Plain tactics for this fight. Soldiers stopped forming shield walls. This was how war was done in the North Morhor Plain, and this was how one needed to fight the Marantaur. The Ifloract came up from the Depths of Flame, and the Mokror and Edhrine came from their ruined ranks. The Marantaur swung his maces not far from the ground. Of all the troops, the spiders fared best. The small size made them difficult targets for the Marantaur, yet they were mowed down when the Marantaur swung his mace mere inches over of the ground. Additionally, the Marantaur usually shook the spiders off. They did little damage to the beast, but they still survived the best. With the Ifloract came some living flames, ready to burn down the Marantaur. The few Edhormond spearmen used their shields only to guard themselves, as they knew the weakness of shield walls. Spiders crowded behind the shields, waiting for their next chances of attack.

"I see you know your weaknesses, now," the Marantaur bellowed.

"I see that you still see yourself above all else," the Edhrine countered.

The Marantaur began to go into a fit of rage.

"Maybe you need one of my furry friends to calm you down," mocked the Mokror.

"Flame shall burn that fur that is all over you," heckled the Ifloract.

"You do not see your weaknesses, fools!" the Marantaur shouted as he charged toward the Ifloract. The Ifloract opened his invisible cloak and out erupted flames. The living flames added to the inferno. The Edhrine moved into position with the Mokror behind the Marantaur, not knowing what to expect. The Marantaur's fur caught fire, and he raged more. He seemed, however, unaffected by the flames. "Die!" the Marantaur screamed.

Joseph had a flashback to the centaur servant doing just that, and it was all too similar. Joseph recalled how he killed the centaur who had picked up Klokar's axe. He was a somewhat easy kill because he was being irrational. That centaur died in a fit of rage. "Hey, how helpless are you, mindless boar! You think you're so strong! Yet, you can't even scratch us!" Joseph instigated.

The Marantaur stopped trying to hit the living flames and the Ifloract with his maces and turned to Joseph and his duo of Edhormond. "You...will...DIE!" he screamed and charged towards them. Joseph and his friends did not move. Instead, the Eye pointed his spear at the Marantaur's left eye. Anvil and Joseph backed off, and the Eye stayed. The Marantaur collided with the spear, but it hit the Marantaur's hard skin and flew to the Eye's right, landing in a bush. The Eye pulled out his bow and drew an arrow back. "You really think that would slay me," thundered the Marantaur as his maces came from both sides into the Eye's head before the Eye could get off his shot. The Edhrine watched in horror as the Eye fell. Yellow mist poured out from the neck and the stone became nonliving. The Eye was a highly developed Edhormond spearman, and now, he was slain. The Marantaur eyed Joseph and promised, "That will also be your fate."

Fighting resumed, and Joseph and Anvil took part using the Eye's bow. They managed to pull it from the Eye's remains when the Marantaur wasn't looking. Anvil used the Eye's bow and Joseph used his semi-machine crossbow. Neither got a hit on the Marantaur. The Errorunsai put up a good fight, and the Marantaur sped north once the fight became a stalemate. This was not the same Marantaur that Joseph watched fighting in the North Morhor Plain the first time. His strength had intensified. Now, he could lift a finger and render a small squad of soldiers dead, not to mention ones associated with the Errorunsai. The Edhrine and the Mokror stayed and helped rebuild the Ifloract's armies. They buried the dead in shallow graves since there was no time to make a real graveyard. The Errorunsai held a meeting in the Depths of Flame on the lowest floor. Joseph had no idea how the Errorunsai, especially the Edhrine, under armor or robes could handle the heat. Joseph wore only his cape, armor, and light clothing, and he was sweating a noticeable puddle on the floor. They had three allies now, but Joseph knew that was not enough. He knew the North Morhor Plain tribesmen were good soldiers for fighting the Marantaur. They were used to being around and fighting alongside and against him.

13

The Dead Rise

Joseph went to the town in front of Edhormon and talked to the former soldiers among the North Morhor Plain tribesmen. All were in favor of helping, but they all agreed they weren't organized enough. Someone had to lead them, establish a chain of command, and keep the army functioning. After speaking with the Edhrine, Joseph knew he was best positioned to be that someone. He became the head of the new North Morhor Military, and the tribesmen agreed that upon their return to the North Morhor Plain, they would form one nation and keep it together. Joseph got everything ready for the military. He started with troop armor. At first, he planned a frontal spike like the one on Mohraight helmets, but then he changed it to a frontal blade, like Edhormond spearmen, Sorwondian wall guards, and the helmets of the tribe that fought alongside the Marantaur on Joseph's first visit. He determined these men would make good polearm skirmishers, which means they fight with spears and small shields or pikes without a phalanx. Joseph made a sub faction flag for the North Morhor Military. He also added spikes to the standard-issue shield for the spearmen.

Unlike most armies, the North Morhor Military used different heads for spears and pikes.

Once organized, the North Morhor Military needed generals, and Joseph technically had no role even though he virtually created the military. Soon, Joseph oversaw the North Morhor Military. Joseph drilled the soldiers and drilled them more. The soldiers despised this, but Joseph knew tough training meant the difference between life and death. In the rebellion, that was one mistake Joseph made. He didn't go hard enough on his men. Joseph also knew that it could also mean the difference between defeat and victory, and the difference between a village liberated and a village massacred and looted.

After getting the North Morhor Military ready, Joseph stepped down as General of the army to instead become the commander of an elite unit. He did not want to miss the combat at the front lines by sitting in an office, plotting. Anvil stayed with Joseph and joined the elite unit. With Joseph and Anvil were some anonymous elites with code names. They were Liberator-1, Liberator-2, and Liberator-3. Liberator-1 was like the Eye, but less skilled. The Eye could not be matched in skill by anyone. Liberator-1 hid in bushes and spied on or harassed the enemy. Liberator-2 specialized in clearing trenches, especially ones filled with archers or crossbowmen. Liberator-3 was a good hand-to-hand combatant, just an expert version of any soldier.

With the North Morhor Military organized and ready, the Three went back to planning where to strike or defend next. However, the Three could not agree on where to move the troops.

"After the attack at the Ifloract's, the Marantaur will go to New Sorwond. He moved across the board last time," the Edhrine commented.

The Mokror countered, "No, I sense something is up. He is confident after killing the Eye. I feel that his forces will move back into the South Morhor Mountains and attack again."

"You are both wrong! They will strike the Mokror next. Do you see it? They struck Joseph and me. Next is the Mokror, and then perhaps the Edhrine!" the Ifloract predicted.

After much discussion, they settled on stationing the troops in all three of the suspected locations with easy transportation to either of the other two locations. That way they could repel an attack in any location. Edhormond spearmen took residence in New Sorwond. The Ifloract's pikes made lines around the South Morhor Mountains to prevent an attack on either the Ifloract or the Mokror. The Mokror's spiders backed up the Ifloract's pikes, patrolling the lines by walking under the extended pikes and scouting ahead.

"Edhrine! They are coming!" an Edhormond exclaimed as he burst into the Edhrine's room. The Edhrine had chosen to come in person to New Sorwond alongside his troops to take part in any one-versus-one duel. He had gotten word that the remaining militia men had champions for dueling, which could easily take most generals in battle. Of course, if they asked for the leader, the Edhrine could come and win in a few moves. Nobody beat an Errorunsin in a one versus one duel.

"I am on my way," the Edhrine responded. He walked out onto the street and began to increase the New Sorwondian morale. His troops weren't affected by it, but these men were. "Go! Fight! But remember, you were born first to die to free Sorwond, and you were born like many others to die to free us all from the Marantaur!" encouraged the Edhrine.

New Sorwondian soldiers carried this message to all the soldiers in the area. That was step one. Next, the Edhrine looked out and saw waves of militia men approaching from the east with some strange apparitions. "What are those?" the Edhrine asked.

"I don't know sir," a nearby New Sorwondian soldier responded.

"Perhaps they are using a form of sorcery to make their numbers appear greater. They may be using more formed apparitions in their lines to appear like extra soldiers," suggested a nearby Edhormond archer.

The Edhrine called for juggernauts to position themselves alongside berserkers. The big guns were needed for this. He decided to wait for the inevitable call for a duel. "If I am needed, I'll go out there and fight," the Edhrine told the men around him.

"I wish to see the leader!" demanded a militia champion.

This was the Edhrine's time. "As you wish," replied a New Sorwondian soldier, smirking.

The Edhrine came forward, and the champion backed up a little.

"Woah! You wanted this," teased an Edhormond spearman.

As the Edhrine prepared for his fight, the berserkers and juggernauts had done little in their charge. They mostly got hit by the machine crossbows that were on the other side. It made no sense. How did they get those? "How about this?" the Edhrine said to the champion. "If you surrender now, you become a prisoner and must explain why there are machine crossbows on your side. Understood?"

"I accept," replied the overmatched champion, who was disarmed and captured by the soldiers.

"Now hold up your end of the deal," the Edhrine demanded, pushing his longsword into the champion's neck.

"I...ack...know...ack," the champion gasped.

"Okay, okay, stop choking" heckled the Edhrine, withdrawing his sword.

"The undead," the champion muttered.

"What?" questioned the Edhrine. "Undead?"

"From the east. They come from mountains of burial. At least, that is where they rise. They come from all over," the champion said, now speaking in nonsense.

"Keep explaining!" the Edhrine demanded.

The champion responded, again, "From the east. They come from mountains of buri—" The Edhrine ran out of patience and decapitated the champion.

"That went well," laughed the Edhrine as he dislodged his sword and watched the champion collapse until he was lying on the floor. "Get this buried," the Edhrine ordered.

With a quiet splash, Joseph landed. The Edhormond raft landed on the shore of one of the Mohraight River's tributaries. He and his elite team disembarked. They rushed up to New Sorwondian defenses on the edge of the Centaur Woods and saw Mohraight and Nacreato ships behind them in the distance, more Edhormond rafts, and all sorts of ships loaded with troops from other locations coming in. Joseph rushed up the shore with Anvil, Liberator-1, Liberator-2, and Liberator-3. Once they reached the streets, they continued east and came upon the front lines. Troops advanced across open ground only to be mowed down by machine ballistae. "Are those machine crossbows on the other side? Since when did the enemy have machine crossbows?" Joseph questioned.

They continued their trek eastward and came upon an enemy trench. "Trenches? I'll take care of this," bragged Liberator-2. Liberator-2 pulled out a sack of throwing axes and searched for cover. He found some on the side, the group following closely.

They crawled through a thorn bush. "Seriously? We could have gotten through the clearing over there!" protested Liberator-1.

"Be quiet!" Joseph ordered.

Soon the elites reached the edge of the enemy trench. Liberator-2 stepped forward and started throwing his axes in, laying prone so the enemy could not see his head. They just saw an arm throwing axes. Liberator-2 heard screams, as expected. Suddenly, there was a loud whoosh! A misty apparition came from the trench. It was a Nacreato machine cross-bower. Liberator-2 stood, and saw that behind the first ghost was another ghostly machine cross-bower being dismantled by some wind. The mist that made him up was being blown away to the east.

"Reeessst," the dying soul faintly said.

The elites jumped out of their cover and got around Liberator-2. They looked in the trench and saw militia men and these souls fighting side by side. The elites looked to their left and saw the machine ballistae and banners of New Sorwond. This was it. The elites jumped into the trench and began fighting. Soon crossbow bolts were flying in the elites' direction.

"Liberator-3, get your shield up!" Liberator-2 screamed.

Liberator-3's small shield could not hold back the bolts. "AHH!" Liberator-3 yelled and fell to the ground, taking a bolt to the knee. He then took another bolt to the head. He was dead.

The elites had no time to waste. They ran forward and took Liberator-3's spear. One of them threw it forward, killing a militia man. Liberator-2 threw an axe, putting a soul to rest. The elites ran forward, trying to clear the trench. Joseph and his crew continued running down the trench, killing enemies. They encountered New Sorwondian and Sorwondian wraiths, now fighting side by side. Soon, a thrown spear ended Liberator-2, leaving just Joseph, Liberator-1, and Anvil.

"We can't survive. We need to retreat," Liberator-1 warned.

Joseph and Anvil agreed, and they started to retreat, carefully watching for javeliners and cross-bowers behind them. As they were running, a loud crack thundered out. Liberator-1 fell. Behind them, they saw a Traste soldier's wraith. Joseph knew Traste developed a new weapon, but he did not expect this. It was a wooden weapon that looked like a paddle. The soldier held it with two hands, his right on the paddle part and his left on the handle. He held it with the tip of the handle facing the target. When firing, the soldier pulled a rod on the underside backward, and a small metal hammer on the top hammered what seemed to be gunpowder. This fired a projectile through the hollow handle and out to the target. The weapon was one-use, though. After firing, the Traste soldier's weapons burnt up from the gunpowder. Joseph and Anvil escaped to the nearest New Sorwondian city and informed the officials that Joseph's elite team was vanquished.

As Joseph returned from the front lines, he received news that the soldiers in the trenches won the battle. "The enemy is defeated!" a New Sorwondian messenger announced. News spread that the battle was won and Joseph retuned to Edhormon.

"How do those souls form?" asked the Edhrine during a meeting that the Three and Joseph had back at Edhormon.

"Let's not leave anything to chance and run an experiment," said Joseph. "Does anyone have corpses available?"

"I do," the Mokror replied. Soon, the Mokror had an experiment running on her land. There was a buried corpse, an unburied corpse, a buried corpse killed in battle that was retrieved from New Sorwond, and an unburied corpse killed in battle.

"Let's see who becomes a wraith," uttered Joseph as the Three and Joseph waited by the corpses, ready to kill any number of wraiths that rose. None of the corpses had actual weapons near them, but a stick was placed nearby to see if the wraith would stay unarmed or pick up the weapon.

After a week, nothing happened. "What if these souls spread their curse of unrest to the resting dead," the Edhrine said. He had an already risen soul brought in. That captured soul immediately went to the two unburied corpses and reached straight into them.

"Okay, so souls can reach into corpses," the Mokror confirmed. The soul then pulled a soul out of the corpses, yanking it from the corpse. The risen souls and the captured one argued over the weapon. All moved as if some horrible pain flowed through their bodies.

"We have what we need," said the Edhrine. "Give them their second deaths." Joseph gladly put the souls to rest.

The Edhrine continued, "We learned what we need to know. All corpses anywhere must be buried as quickly as possible."

After the experiment, the Ifloract asked, "We have four allies. New Sorwond, Nacreato, Mohraight, and now Traste. Should we change the flag?"

The Edhrine firmly answered, "No. The Traste government explicitly said that our alliance with them is not with New Sorwond, Mohraight, or Nacreato. It's just with us, and it's secret, too."

"Okay," said the Ifloract, "so we keep the three rune in the top right corner."

The Edhrine replied, "The 'three rune' is not correct terminology. The only runes I know of are Sohror (0), Worhiot (1), Borcor (2), Ofor (3), and Aortar (4)."

"Whatever, your Edhormond Runes are complicated," the Ifloract scoffed. "Anyway, I wonder how the Traste man with that new weapon died."

After the meeting, Traste officials met with the Three and introduced their new weapon, the moste. They explained how the weapon worked. A projectile is loaded into the barrel, and the weapon is aimed. Once ready to fire, the wielder pulls the handle back and the hammer on top slams on some gunpowder, causing a propellant explosion that launched a shot capable of piercing heavy armor. However, the explosion causes the moste to burn up in one's hands, so a soldier must retreat after firing and get another moste to shoot again. The Traste officials explained that it was okay if New Sorwond used it, but New Sorwond must pretend that they made the moste to prevent it being traced to Traste.

The Edhrine brought the deal to New Sorwondian top officials and it was accepted. New Sorwondians called the moste by a different name, the Handheld Gunpowder Cannon (HGC). New Sorwondian HGC training camps began filling up. Few ended up in the military as HGC men, so those who did were considered elites. New Sorwond started selling "their" invention, which was okay by the deal, to Mohraight and Nacreato. Very few knew it came from Traste. Joseph himself learned to use an HGC, or moste, but he did not get too far into its training because he did not like that it was only for one use. He couldn't get more if he was behind enemy lines or in an enemy trench. Nonetheless, Joseph always carried a moste with him since it was a powerful, armor-piercing weapon.

"So, the enemy has undead on his side," the Edhrine pondered aloud, "What are we going to do about that?"

Joseph responded, "We do know, at least, that we need to bury or at least lock up corpses. Nonetheless, we need to figure out what motivates the dead. Do the dead have their living will controlling them, or are they possessed? What motivates them to kill their fellow living soldiers and fight alongside enemies. We saw undead New Sorwondian soldiers fighting against their living comrades and alongside old Sorwondians. No living New Sorwondian would do that without a considerably high bribe, if even."

The Three and Joseph conversed for a while longer, discussing possible motivations. The suggestions ranged from bribes to threats, but nobody was sure.

14

The Siege of New Sorwond

Joseph went to his room in Edhormon and laid on the straw bed in his wagon. Anvil stood inside and prepared food for Joseph's breakfast. Joseph was sleeping when Anvil woke him. Based on the lack of light coming from the small window at the top of his tall room, Joseph could tell it was still nighttime.

"One of my brothers came down from the upper floor and informed me that the Three want to meet with you," said Anvil.

"Alrighty," chimed Joseph.

They went through the labyrinth and up the steps. Two Edhormond spearmen stood guarding at the top. "Good night," said Joseph. The Edhormond replied with a polite nod. It seemed odd to tell someone good night when they weren't going to sleep, but it was normal in Edhormon. The Edhormond didn't sleep. Joseph reached the Chamber of Meeting where the Three and he always met. Joseph took his seat across from the Edhrine's platform, and the other of the Three also took their places.

"I called an emergency meeting because of some disturbing news I got from a ring of spies I have all over the place," stated the Edhrine.

"Do you actually have a ring of spies?" the Ifloract asked.

"It is complicated. The point is: Souls are rising in the Mohraight Graveyard. Mokror, you should probably get your spiders feasting. It will get some of those corpses out of the rocks and into somewhere safe. Good news: They don't know where to find a target. Bad news: The enemy will likely try to get to them and inform them of the Mokror's home."

"I'll go help get rid of that soul army," proclaimed Joseph, checking to make sure he had his shortswords and then looking up.

"Go," said the Edhrine.

The Mokror also volunteered. "I'm coming for obvious reasons. This is my home we're talking about. There is one problem with burying the corpses. My spiders and I need to figure out a way to continue eating, though. We can't eat all corpses at once, or we'll starve later. If we bury them, I'll be the one person who will need to dig them up. We need to figure out something that will keep us eating."

Joseph departed in his wagon alongside an Edhormond barge. Anvil rowed, while the Mokror relaxed. Joseph watched the ten oars on two of the sides of the square Edhormond barge row in unison. Edhormond barges were interesting. They had oars on all four sides, but only two sides ever worked at the same time. The oars on the two sides not in use were locked into an upward position, pointing toward the sky. There were always a few towers and spears poking up from the barge, too. The small barrier that went around the outer edge of the barge could not guard everything. That was why the towers had heavy armor.

"Undead!" the Mokror announced.

Joseph snapped back into reality and pulled out his two weapons. The Mokror took out a battle horn and blew. Edhormond steel bows instantly came out of most of the archer holes in the barge. These soldiers were ready.

A shout of gibberish came from some rocks ahead, and souls of sailors ran up and down the rocks. Soon, crossbow bolts were flying.

"I didn't know these corpses had crossbows!" the Mokror shouted.

"Well, don't you drag them inland?" Joseph asked.

"No, my spiders do."

Joseph and the Mokror countered with semi-machine crossbows and small throwing daggers.

The Mokror grumbled, "Dang, I wish these went a little farther!" after her eighth thrown dagger landed in the water.

"Anvil, bring us in a little more," Joseph instructed. Soon the group was closer, doing what they could against the enemy with Joseph's crossbow and the Mokror's daggers. Meanwhile, the crushing numbers of archers in the Edhormond barge hammered away, getting tens of kills every five seconds. The archers fired in unison at the rocks.

The fighting raged on, and the resistance faded. The barge pushed towards the shore of the rocks with the archers looking for the sources of the occasional crossbow bolt that bounced off the Edhormond steel armor. Joseph's wagon and the barge landed at roughly the same time. Right upon landing, ramps dropped and Edhormond spearmen marched off. Joseph and his passengers disembarked their wagon and attached the wheels. Once completed, Joseph attached the horses to the front. Edhormond soldiers quickly surrounded the wagon. The wagon stood out against the waves of Edhormond steel. While Anvil was steering, Joseph and the Mokror nailed steel plates onto the wagon. Joseph did not need a flaming arrow hitting his personal vehicle and it burning to the ground. Joseph and the force with him searched the rocks, finished off the souls, and got back out to sea. They repeated this process until they wiped out most of the souls. After they finished, some of the Mokror's spiders took over and Joseph left. With the objective completed, they returned to Edhormon.

After several uneventful months, a day patrol spotted militia skirmishers in the outer woods. The patrolmen pretended not to see them, and they returned and informed command. A meeting was called in the Klokar's Palace command center. The Three, Joseph, his assistants, and generals from New Sorwond, the Edhormond, the Ifloract's troops, and even the Mokror's spiders attended.

The Edhrine announced, "I am afraid that enemy skirmishers were spotted in the southern edge of the Centaur Woods. The purpose of this meeting is to make an educated guess as to what that means and respond accordingly."

A New Sorwondian general stood and spoke. "I believe that this is preparation for an invasion of New Sorwond and must be dealt with immediately. New Sorwondian elite skirmishers should eliminate the threat to prevent the enemy from scouting our defenses."

"Nonsense!" scoffed a fiery soul from the Ifloract's army. "I was created to be a tactician and I believe that this is an enemy patrol to make sure our activity is where they want it. I do think they will invade, but we require a different strategy to make the most out of this. If we pretend this never happened, we can strengthen our inner defenses. Let them think we are open and weak. They attack, and we destroy them. If they know they were caught, they will pull back and think up something else. We can lower the finite numbers of their army to nothing if we plan for their attack. If we push them out, they will attack elsewhere where we aren't expecting them."

An argument followed. The Edhrine calmed everyone and held a vote. The Ifloract's army won. Inner defense of New Sorwond was to be strengthened.

Soon, the speculation was confirmed. New Sorwondians stalked the enemy militia men and located a siege party. The besiegers began the march to New Sorwond, preparing to enter through the "hole" in New Sorwond's defenses. The trap was ready, and the prey was moving right into it.

"On alert, everyone! On alert! The first city is in sight!" an enemy militia commander announced.

A New Sorwondian strike force lay prone on a cliff overlooking the enemy. "Steady!" Some men tensed. "Steady," the strike force commander repeated. "Just a little farther," the commander muttered under his breath. The front lines of the siege party had not yet reached the edge of the trap. The commander wanted his force to rain down on as many men as possible. When the front lines reached the edge, "Now!" the commander screamed. The trap was sprung. Strike force soldier soldiers ran to the edge of the cliff and jumped off. They were attached via ropes to the soldiers behind them, the soldiers behind those soldiers, and down the train to some specialized spools. Soldiers repelled down, and the cables suspended them just above the ground. Soldiers used their daggers to quickly cut themselves free and started fighting. As the front lines cut free, the spools in the back let some more string loose, allowing the second lines to cut free without falling to their deaths. The spool let loose more, and even more soldiers joined the fight against the militia. After intense fighting, New Sorwond won.

"Check the corpses to make sure they're dead. Make sure

every single one gets buried, or we could have a bigger problem on our hands!" the strike force commander directed. The commander thought he saw something move. He looked, but it was nothing. He saw it again!

Suddenly, a soul moved up behind the commander and stabbed him with a dagger. "Reeeliieeefff," sighed the soul. The soul pulled the commander's soul out of his corpse.

"Get the corpses secured!" a soldier shouted.

"We need backup!" yelled another.

"Your backup has arrived," announced some HGC men coming in. More came, and the men formed a line. The firing line shot each soul dead.

The commander of the HGC squad came forward from the side of the line. "Good job men," he said, surveying the situation. "What happened here?" he asked, looking at the corpses.

"Some soul was waiting here, and he tried to raise the dead when the siege failed," a strike force soldier reported.

The HGC commander then said, "I'll inform High Command."

"...So, in short, the enemy siege party had a soul with it. When the siege party died, the soul started raising the fallen. This attempt was suppressed by the HGC squad," the HGC commander recounted.

"Very well. High Command will look at this battle to find common strategies used by the enemy," said a New Sorwondian general and the HGC commander departed the meeting room.

High Command conducted another meeting. New Sorwondian staff filled the seats, alongside representatives from the Edhormon, Ifloract's army, Mokror's spiders, Mohraight, and Nacreato.

Joseph cautioned, "This is problematic."

"Indeed, it is," the Edhrine agreed. "We have seen the enemy use a potentially devastating tactic. After the New Sorwondian ambush successfully destroyed the enemy siege party, a soul attempted to raise the fallen besiegers. The soul failed, but if the enemy sends more souls next time, we might not be so lucky."

A New Sorwondian general spoke next, "Perhaps we could make a weapon that eliminated all souls in an area while leaving living beings unharmed."

"I think I know how we could do that," said Joseph, "but it won't be easy. King Salo used sorcery to bend his people, meaning he must have had an altar. He even said he did, but refused to give the location. Maybe we could revert the sorcery that rose the souls and lay them to rest."

15

The Secret in the Ruins

Joseph and a team of New Sorwondian soldiers picked through the rubble of the old Sorwondian city. "Over here!" a soldier hollered. Joseph and the others ran over. "I found the entryway into Salo's bunker. This is where he came out from and surrendered. Let's see if this door will open." He gave the small wooden door a shove and the door barely vibrated.

"That won't work. Maybe..." Joseph mused. He sent a soldier for a torch. The soldier rode on a horse to a nearby New Sorwondian camp to get a torch.

He returned a while later. "Here, sir," the soldier said as he dismounted his horse.

Joseph turned to the door and lit it on fire. He found that the door was almost a foot thick, and had a six-inch-thick deadbolt lock keeping it closed. However, it was still wooden and the torch was successful.

"Looks like Salo closed the door behind him when he came out," noted a soldier, "which means he didn't want anyone seeing what was down here."

Joseph warned, "Sorcery is powerful. It controls thousands,

raises the dead, and more. There's a pretty good chance that it can guard a bunker, too. I suggest caution."

Joseph and his team moved into the bunker and descended a staircase. They searched a few rooms using the light from the torch they used to burn down the door. Most rooms were barracks, offices, and the like. At the end of the long hallway that connected the rooms was a stone door.

A soldier joked, "There's no burning that one down."

"There is not," chuckled a cold, soft voice. "No one goes there."

"Salo is dead! We killed your master. Allow us to pass," Joseph demanded.

"If you killed Salo, then I will avenge him. However, he is not my master," the voice replied.

"Who are you?" Joseph asked.

"I am your death!" What looked like the soul of some Sorwondian warlord materialized before them, just in front of the stone door. "Are you ready to regret coming down here?"

"I'm good with not regretting it," Joseph countered, drawing his shortswords. He charged and stabbed the soul, but it didn't move.

The soul chuckled again, "As you can see, that won't work."

The soldiers and Joseph retreated down the hallway, but the soul came forward. Joseph couldn't lay this soul to rest. How would he be able to get by? Wait, maybe he didn't have to kill it. Joseph starting walking towards the soul, noticing how it had not drawn its axe.

The soul drew its weapon and said, "Nice try!" Joseph didn't stop walking forward. "Be gone!" bellowed the soul, starting to back away.

"You are not real. You are nothing but an apparition, made by

Salo to guard this place. The only power you have is to make the afraid turn back, but I know what you are!" Joseph declared.

"No! NOO!" the apparition screeched, as it faded back towards the door, an invisible wind dissipating the gray mist that composed the apparition.

"What was that?" a soldier asked.

Joseph replied, "That was an apparition. It isn't real, and once you realize it's not real, it doesn't even have the power to exist."

The soldiers arrived back at the stone door. Joseph tried to open it, but it was locked.

"What's new? Let me handle this," bragged a soldier. He pulled out a long, thin dagger and wedged it in between the one side of door and the wall. Finding nothing, he moved to the other side of the door. His dagger caught on something about halfway up. "Here's the lock." He tried using the dagger to remove the lock, but to no avail. Then, he removed an axe that was strapped to his back and put away the thin dagger. He used the axe to break the wooden lock and opened the door.

"Good work," said Joseph. They entered a large chamber with an altar in the middle. Two statues holding swords were on pedestals flanking the altar.

"Um, how does this work?" a soldier asked.

"Not to worry. We just need to secure this place. Someone else will use the altar," another soldier replied. The soldiers searched the bunker and found something else. They found a door down a small side hallway. A soldier opened it. There was a balcony overlooking a huge room. Chains dangled down from the ceiling, and devices of torture sat on the floors. There was one gate out of this place, and it was open. The chains were unlocked, and the restraints on the torture devices open.

"No. It can't be," Joseph exclaimed. "This is the place where King Salo tortured people to insanity. He created the army of the tortured and released the army during the Siege of Sorwond."

"Oh, yeah. You were there," a soldier muttered.

The soldiers and Joseph continued securing the area. Once they were done, reinforcements arrived. The soldiers who helped Joseph secure the area left for a nearby camp. The reinforcements went in and stood guard. Among the reinforcements was none other than the Edhrine.

"Greetings, Joseph," the Edhrine said, stepping down from his chariot.

"Greetings," Joseph replied.

The Edhrine and Joseph walked down the steps into the bunker and to the altar. The Edhrine inspected the altar. "There are runes on here that make this altar capable of only one spell...a will control spell. It's likely the one Salo used. If I can remove the runes, though, I'll be able to do my own things. Now, this rune makes the will control spell easier to do. Without the rune, I can do any spell, but it'll be harder." The Edhrine concentrated. Yellow mist slowly started to form around the runes. The Edhrine concentrated harder, and more yellow mist formed. Suddenly, the runes fell off the altar. The Edhrine released his concentration and the yellow mist gradually went away. The Edhrine took the runes and placed them in the hallway and returned to the altar. "Lay to rest the risen dead!" the Edhrine shouted. Yellow mist started to form on top of the altar. Then, the mist subsided.

Joseph asked, "What is it?"

"The altar wants something in return for this spell. It wants...it wants enough weapons," the Edhrine said.

"Enough weapons? How many exactly are enough?"

"I can't give you an exact number, but I'll know when we have enough on the altar. Sorcery works in strange ways."

Joseph and the Edhrine began calling for weapons from New Sorwond. Wagons arrived with more and more spears, swords, bows, and arrows. Soldiers rushed the weapons down to Joseph and the Edhrine. Joseph and the Edhrine then put them on the altar.

"That's enough," the Edhrine said. Soldiers passed the word around. Weapons stopped coming.

Joseph exclaimed, "That's a lot of weapons!"

The Edhrine recited the phrase, "Lay to rest the risen dead!" The altar began to emit yellow mist. The Edhrine repeated the phrase, "Lay to rest the risen dead!" More yellow mist came up. The weapons on the altar began to evaporate. "Lay to rest the risen dead!" the Edhrine shouted one, last time.

A voice responded, "The souls you seek to lay to rest were risen not by this altar. Only the altar that rose them can lay them to rest." The last of the weapons evaporated, and then all the yellow mist went into the cold stone of the altar.

"So, we just wasted three New Sorwondian weapon stockpiles for nothing," Joseph groaned. "Great! Not like their command will be mad or anything."

The Edhrine consoled him, "Well, at least we tried, but for now, the souls are going to be laid to rest by weapons only."

"We did learn something, though," Joseph remarked. "We know that Salo didn't have any part in raising the dead, and the only spell he did here was will control. So, we have to search elsewhere for another altar."

With that, Joseph, the Edhrine, and Anvil traveled back to Edhormon on Joseph's wagon.

16

Unfinished Business

Joseph was back in his room. It was a few months since he and the Edhrine tried to use the altar to lay the dead to rest. The past few months had been relatively uneventful. Both sides of the war were trying to build strength rather than fight. Joseph awoke after being startled. He heard an Edhormond soldier speaking, "... so, you need to go to the area south of the Centaur Woods, on the Sacred River." Joseph assumed the soldier's first attempt to wake him had failed and the soldier did not realize that Joseph was still asleep. Joseph probably woke up towards the end of his message. He hoped he hadn't missed anything important. The soldier was still speaking, "Figure out who these people are and why they are assembling. Again, the orders are from the Edhrine, and he asked for you to come to his chamber before you set out." Joseph put on his gear and went to the Edhrine's chamber.

Joseph entered the familiar room, which had a table, chairs, and the Edhrine's platform. The Edhrine was facing the other way, standing on his platform. Without turning around, the Edhrine began speaking, "Greetings. I see that you arrived."

"Yes, I have. I believe I am to go to the Sacred River," Joseph replied.

"That is correct. As the messenger no doubt told you that an army has assembled there and belongs to an unknown faction. I advise caution. That will be all." With that, Joseph said goodbye and went to his wagon.

Joseph sat in the back of his wagon, watching Anvil steer. He imagined the Eye standing there, going over Edhormond battle tactics or polishing his gear. Joseph wished the Eye was still alive. He knew, though, that the magic that could raise the dead made them slaves to their master. Joseph didn't want the Eye to be a mindless soul. Joseph thought about getting a new assistant for tactical plans. He decided that he might ask the Edhrine after this mission...if he survived. This army could be hostile to the Three.

Joseph met with a New Sorwondian army, and together, they marched toward the site of this strange new faction. The army's leaders talked to Joseph about plans should the enemy attempt to ambush them or be otherwise hostile. Soon, the army and Joseph arrived. There, in the hills, was a massive army of soldiers with gleaming iron armor. It was nightfall, so small fires were set in the ranks of soldiers to make sure that the soldiers could see. Whatever weapons they carried lay hidden. What amazed Joseph was that the soldiers were standing at attention and it appeared that they were this way for a long time. It simply wasn't possible. Suddenly, Joseph saw a flash of brown and white to his right, which made him instantly turn. He saw a scout, in the same gleaming armor as the other soldiers, holding a torch. Joseph now understood. The scout saw them coming. He signaled with the torch to the army of soldiers to stand at attention and look impressive.

A voice called out from behind Joseph. Joseph whirled around and pulled out his swords, finding a soldier without a helmet with two soldiers escorting him. The two soldiers pulled out loaded crossbows and aimed at Joseph. "Easy! Stand down," directed the soldier without a helmet. The soldiers put the crossbows away, and Joseph put his swords away, too.

"Apologies. You surprised me," Joseph said.

"Do not worry. I don't blame you. Anyway, I see you are a skilled skirmisher. I am General Peter of the Sentinels of Monfor. And you are?"

"I am Joseph." As Joseph was about to speak again, he heard a distant clanking. He recognized the sound. The Edhormond were here for some reason. "Why are the Edhormond coming?"

General Peter raised an eyebrow, "Edhormond? What are they doing here? Men, get ready for some violence, but don't throw the first punch!"

Joseph was confused. "You speak of the Edhormond as if they are enemies."

General Peter replied, "Of course! Centuries ago, there was a dispute between us and the Edhrine that resulted in bloodshed. For an Errorunsin, that wasn't too long ago. The Edhrine likely still has a problem with us."

Joseph understood. The Edhormond were not here to say hello. They were here to kill. Soon, the Edhormond army arrived. At the front stood the Edhrine himself.

"Greetings, gentlemen. As this Sentinel general likely told you, we have...unfinished business," expressed the Edhrine. "Joseph, you do not need to get involved, unless if you would like to help us, please do." The Edhrine took a step back and faded into his army. He ordered his troops using the Edhormond language. The Edhormond pulled their spears out of their holders and shields from their holders. The Edhormond raised their shields, pointed their spears forward, and began to charge toward the Sentinels.

"You are with them!" the general shouted, looking at Joseph. He turned to some men, "Seize him!" Two Sentinels ran from the crowd with loaded crossbows.

Joseph had no intention of surrendering, but no intention of killing Sentinels. Joseph picked up a rock and threw it hard at one Sentinel. The Sentinel fell, unconscious. Joseph ran at the second soldier and thrust the pommel of one of his shortswords right into his face. The second man fell, too.

The Edhrine stood behind his army. He watched the Sentinels fall as his army ran into them. He saw some still alive on the ground. That wouldn't do. He shouted to a few Edhormond with him, "Get a squad to deal with the survivors!" Following his command, a group of Edhormond spearmen finished off the wounded enemy. The Edhrine peered into the crowd of Sentinels. They had their cloaks at their feet. The Edhrine knew the Sentinels traveled in small groups dressed in the cloaks. The cloaks concealed their armor and made detecting them extremely difficult.

Joseph was now fighting with two thick branches against several Sentinels. The New Sorwondian army was fighting, too. Joseph knew that in time, the Sentinels would have to surrender. He saw the waves of Edhormond soldiers ramming into anyone and anything in their path. Some Sentinels tried to run, only for the Edhormond to catch up and stab and trample them. Joseph then saw something disturbing. Edhormond marched down the ranks of enemy dead in the waves' wake, stabbing the dead just to make sure. The Edhrine took no prisoners. Joseph snapped back to alertness, and quickly found a Sentinel to knock out.

Joseph didn't need to make a new enemy if he didn't have to.

The few remaining Sentinels attempted to fire at the Edhormond with crossbows, only to be crushed by the wave of death that was the Edhormond line. Soon, the remaining Sentinels surrendered. The Edhrine had plans for that. Joseph watched as the Edhormond line drew nearer. He saw Sentinels surrendering. They would likely be okay, he thought. Joseph was wrong. The Edhrine himself came, sword drawn, and went down the line. He decapitated all except one random Sentinel, who he stabbed in the chest instead. The Edhrine then went to General Peter.

"What do you want, Edhrine?" General Peter snapped.

"I do not require anything that you can give me. Maybe I should just do it right now."

"Do wha—" the general began to ask, but was interrupted by the Edhrine's blade slicing his legs from his body. Then, the Edhrine finished the general off by decapitating him.

The Edhrine and his army began marching away with Joseph and New Sorwondians following them. Joseph ended up in an Edhormond chariot with the Edhrine. "Why did you kill them all?" Joseph asked. "Was it for revenge?"

The Edhrine snarled, "No! I avenged the people they murdered. Here is the story: They were just another faction some three hundred years ago. That was, until they tried to set camp on Edhormond land. We kindly asked them to leave, so they went to the very edge of our land and camped there. I posted soldiers to watch from the shadows, just in case. It was a good thing I did. We got word from the scouts that they were moving toward a nearby outpost. The scouts went in for a closer look and never came back. Other scouts witnessed the Sentinels throwing them into a huge fire, burning them to death. Next came the massacre. The Sentinels reached the outpost and murdered every Edhormond in sight. We did nothing to provoke them, yet they killed. It started a war, until the Sentinels went into hiding. That was when I learned the Sentinels became the Sentinels of Monfor. I started looking there, but failed to find them. Little did I know, the Sentinels used cloaks to disguise themselves, and many passed my armies and search parties unnoticed. They fled Monfor until I left, and then they returned to Monfor. Twenty-five years later, they attacked again. This time, they had managed to convince a large group of factions to fight with them. They came, with their combined strength. I knew we could have won, but I withdrew to the mountains where I reside now, knowing that they would just keep coming and the blood would keep flowing. Now, three centuries later, I had a chance to finish the war."

"Interesting," Joseph replied. "However don't you think holding a gru—"

The Edhrine interrupted, "It's not a grudge. Is seeking justice for hundreds murdered holding a grudge?"

"Well, yes. Also, three centuries may not be very long for you, but for the Sentinels, they could have had a revolution. They could be a completely different group than the one you warred against. The leaders who hated you are surely dead. If they held a grudge for three centuries, then that's just amazing. For you, it's more understandable. You've lived for millennia."

"That is true, but it does not change the fact that they murdered Edhormond."

Joseph spoke again, "Remember, we are fighting a war as it is. We can't fight two at once. Maybe they came to join us. Perhaps they had reasons to fight the One, and you may have obliterated any chance of alliance."

"True," the Edhrine agreed.

Joseph and the Edhrine arrived at Edhormon. As they entered the town, civilians were on the sides of the streets, watching the arrival of the Edhrine, Joseph, and the Edhormond army. Joseph asked the Edhrine how many civilians lived in the Edhormond town.

The Edhrine replied, "There are some fifty thousand people here."

"Fifty thousand? How do you house them in a town like this?"

"Although this place is built like a town, it is more like a city in size," the Edhrine explained. Unexpectedly, a javelin flew out a window toward the Edhrine. When Joseph glanced at the Edhrine, he saw the Edhrine standing with his sword drawn, and the javelin cut clean in half. "Find that assassin!" the Edhrine ordered, and Edhormond ran into the building from where the javelin came. Inside, they found a man hiding, dressed in a cloak. The Edhormond brought him before the Edhrine. "Identify yourself!" the Edhrine demanded. When the assassin remained silent, the Edhrine yanked off his cloak. As soon as the cloak was off, the Edhrine recognized the armor. It was a Sentinel.

"Did you really think that your murderous massacre of our troops would go unnoticed?" the Sentinel asked.

"If you want to see a murderous massacre, why don't you go check the history books, which mention how Sentinels murderously massacred Edhormond," the Edhrine responded. "Take him away!" Two Edhormond dragged the Sentinel away.

17

Trials of Edhormon

The Edhrine stood on his platform, staring at the wall. He needed to put something there to stare at. He spent most of his days staring at this blank wall. The Edhrine had an idea. He removed his sword from his belt and began carving a design. When he was done, he had carved an Ofor rune on the wall. The Ofor rune meant three. He carved the other Edhormond runes around the Ofor, but not as big. In the end, he had a large Ofor in the middle with the other four runes around it, in order. He now had something to look at when he stood on his platform facing away from the door to the room, but more importantly, he had just made something more powerful than all the soldiers one could want.

The Mokror stood in her chamber. Her spiders were talented, but they did not suffice for every need. They could not grasp objects very well. The Mokror planned to change that. She went to the back of her chamber, where body parts of various creatures covered the floor. She didn't understand why people found it disgusting, when they could make many things. The Mokror pieced the parts together into two new creations to start breeding, and after that they would multiply.

The Ifloract floated above his lava pool. He heard of an assassination attempt on the Edhrine, so he assigned some living flames and ashen soldiers to be his bodyguards. He thought about all the materials around him and observed his ashen soldiers. They served their purpose as bodyguards well, but they were not completely loyal nor intelligent. They relied on the living flames for guidance, and him for a leader to be loyal to. He needed a more dedicated bodyguard unit. He floated down into the lava below him and examined the materials in there. He was going to make something...else.

The Marantaur stood in a fortress. It was made of stone, but not like the Edhrine's stone. This stone was deprived of power. All power was in the Marantaur now. The emperor taught him how to remove power from objects. He knew that killing the Eye strengthened him. He just needed to get a bigger army.

"Soul," bellowed the Marantaur, "have you found the Errorunsai's tombs? I know where mine are, but I don't know where in the Dark Mountains the others are located."

"No, sir!" shouted the soul over a nearby windstorm that was getting more intense. "We found the Eye's burial site, but none of the others. The Edhrine made a separate tomb for the Eye rather than give him a place alongside the other Edhormond."

"That was his mistake. We only need the Eye," boasted the Marantaur, chuckling a terrible laugh over his lands.

Joseph finished sharpening his shortswords. He tested the edge on the stone wall. The tip carved a line into the wall. It was good. He looked to his right and saw Anvil adding more Edhormond steel to his hammers to make them heavier. Joseph thought about the Edhrine's demonstration of sorcery at the altar. The Edhrine contacted the altar and asked the altar to do something. While the mission was a failure, it demonstrated the power of the Edhrine. As he thought more about the recent events, based on what the Edhrine told him, the Edhrine was sort of in the right when he massacred the Sentinels even if the Sentinels could have changed over the many years. Joseph assumed that the assassin was sent to send a message to the Edhrine to not to mess with the Sentinels. However, the Edhrine showed the Sentinels not to mess with him. Joseph heard the door to his chamber open. He turned around, putting away his shortswords. An Edhormond soldier stood in the doorway. "The Edhrine wants you to visit his inner chamber." With that, the soldier walked back into the hallway.

Joseph arrived with the Anvil at the Chamber of Meeting. He noticed that the Edhrine had carved runes into the wall behind his platform. From the Chamber of Meeting, Anvil escorted Joseph to the door on the right. Joseph remembered the first time he met the Edhrine that the Edhrine came out of that door with two guards. Anvil opened the door, and Joseph entered the room. In the room, there was something very rare in Edhormon, a window. The Edhrine sat on a raised stone platform looking out the window. There was a sorcery altar in the room with interchangeable rune tablets. Without turning around, the Edhrine called out, "Greetings."

Joseph replied, "Greetings. You would not call me to your inner chamber without reason."

"That is correct. I am going to upgrade your blades."

The Edhrine eyed the keen edge of the blades and noticed that Joseph sharpened them. Joseph handed the blades to the Edhrine and the Edhrine placed them on the sorcery altar. He knelt before the altar and raised his right hand above the altar. Yellow mist emitted from the altar and rose into the air. At that moment, Joseph's blades levitated above the altar.

"Altar of Edhormon, unleash your power into these blades!" the Edhrine declared.

A voice responded, "What augmentation do you seek?"

"I seek an Edhormond blade. I seek a blade of steel and mist!"

"You shall have what you seek! Blades! I command you to be of steel and mist!"

The yellow mist in the room condensed around Joseph's blades, enough where the blades were no longer visible. The yellow mist dissipated a little, and Joseph saw the hilts of his blades were now constructed of Edhormond steel. The mist dissipated more, but not entirely. Joseph realized that the mist was where the blades of his weapons were before.

"There is one more ritual we must do," the Edhrine told Joseph. "The blades will dissipate once they leave Edhormond possession. This is a theft countermeasure. Dead Edhormond will have long poles next to them because the spearheads will dissipate until they are back in Edhormond hands. Since you are not affiliated with me, those blades will not work for you. We must make you affiliated with me, but that is a much longer and more complicated procedure...and it could be painful for everyone in the room if you resist. However, that likely won't happen."

Joseph and the Edhrine went through some hallways until they were on a bridge. Joseph saw cavernous mines all around him. They were easily big enough for the all of the old Sorwondian City's buildings to fit in except for the towering keep. All around, Joseph observed Edhormond with pickaxes. The pickaxes had Edhormond steel handles and yellow mist heads. Joseph and the Edhrine went into a hallway at the other end of the mines. They kept walking straight through a few intersections and turned right. There was a set of large double doors at the end. The Edhrine raised his hand to a shiny stone ball. The ball was polished, but it was dark. It seemed to be a dark colored stone, like obsidian. The ball couldn't be obsidian, though, because nobody could cut it that precisely.

The ball began to glow. Joseph realized that it was a very dark black stained-glass ball. In the center of the sphere, a tiny bit of yellow mist began to form. The Edhrine spoke, "Edhormon, this is your master, the Edhrine! Open the doors to the Hall of Initiation!" The ball's yellow mist began to grow and shrink rapidly, once filling the entire sphere. The doors suddenly opened. It appeared that the Edhrine had used this ball to contact some sort of system named after the place it was in. The Hall of Initiation was a massive room. Unlike the mines, however, it could only fit about three Edhormond barges, rather than all of Sorwond. Also, unlike the mines, the room was cut into a geometric rectangle, not the cave-like shape of the mines. At the end of the room was a pool of yellow mist with a podium behind it, likely for the Edhrine. Around the pool, several tombstone-like rectangular stones stood with runes etched into them.

The Edhrine instructed Joseph to stand near the pool, facing him. "There will be a lot of new Edhormond that I just brought to life being initiated here today. You will be at the front of them. They will march straight here and line up behind you. They will wait, standing, and kneel in unison. Once they are on their knees, you kneel as well. I will perform some sorcery, and then you and the new Edhormond will stand and march straight into the pool. It may appear to be small, but there is room for all of you, and fear not. You can breathe in there."

The new Edhormond marched in through the double doors.

The Edhrine had opened the doors through a glass ball on the lectern atop the podium. Along the sides of the room, ranks of Edhormond soldiers stood, holding their weapons. The new Edhormond marched and positioned themselves behind Joseph. They all had Edhormond armor and weapons, but their visors and spearheads were nonexistent. Inside the visor was nothing. It was just a flat, stone surface. The Edhormond were basically living statues and were extremely efficient warriors. Few saw the flat surface of a face and lived, Joseph guessed. By the sounds, Joseph could tell that the Edhormond knelt when the doors closed. Joseph knelt, too. The Edhrine began his sorcery, "Today, these beings here will be made Edhormond. Edhormon, allow this." The glass ball lit in yellow mist and the mist inside began rapidly expanding and contracting. The Edhrine spoke again, "Proceed into the Mist of Initiation!" Joseph and the new Edhormond rose from their knees and marched forward. Since Joseph was at the front, he went in first.

Inside the pool, Joseph sank. He could breathe, but he couldn't swim upwards. The mist pool was extremely deep. All around him, Joseph saw silhouettes of the new Edhormond through the mist. The mist became thicker as he sank deeper. Joseph heard a voice. He saw his mother, Margaret, in the mist. He saw his younger self, too. The scene in the mist was vivid. His mother was banishing him from the house. The scene disappeared, but a new one appeared behind him. Joseph turned around and saw himself escaping Sorwond, busting through the side gate. The image changed again, and he saw the Old Fort in its earliest stages. The scene shifted again, showing the centaur in the cave. The image shifted another time with the Edhormond surrounding him and his rebels with spears, until the scene shifted to the Siege of Sorwond. He saw ranks of Edhormond soldiers and rebels. The image was more vivid than he could ever imagine.

Joseph heard the Edhrine's voice say to him, "Do you regret anything from this battle?" The Edhrine appeared next to the image. He was not as vivid, partially blocked by the thick mist.

"Only the fallen."

"Do you regret the execution of Salo?" asked the Edhrine. The scene shifted to show Salo and his men in the burning oil.

"I do not."

"Yet you accuse me of holding a grudge against the Sentinels!" shouted the Edhrine's apparition.

"I sought justice for the murders he committed and the torture he forced his people to undergo, and to stop him from continuing! The Sentinels stopped killing Edhormond long ago! You sought to avenge!" scolded Joseph.

The apparition responded again, "You seek justice, I seek to avenge. I see no difference. For me, three centuries does not erase the past! I seek justice, too!" The apparition drew his sword and spoke again, "Yet, you still say I hold a grudge." The apparition tried to bring the sword down on Joseph, but Joseph rolled to the side.

"You are not the Edhrine," bellowed Joseph.

"I am not all of the Edhrine. However, I am part of him!" The apparition tried to slice Joseph's legs from his body, but Joseph allowed himself to sink deeper into the mist, under the blow.

"You are not part of the Edhrine!" exclaimed Joseph. The apparition continued slashing and stabbing at Joseph. "You may be part of the Edhrine, but you do not control him, and you will not control me."

The apparition put away his sword. "You have passed the trial. This is the Edhrine."

The Edhrine disappeared, and Joseph sensed himself rising at a fast pace. His head broke the surface of the pool, and he rose higher, stopping just above the pool. The Edhrine spoke, "You are now with the Edhormond!" Joseph looked around and saw the new Edhormond floating around him, except for two who crawled out of the pool, having failed their trials. He and the other new Edhormond fell into the mist again, but stopped once their feet were submerged. Joseph felt a solid surface under his boots, and he walked out of the pool. The other Edhormond walked out of the pool, too. The Edhormond in the room came out of the ranks and the room was full of conversations and noise. Joseph ascended the stairs to the podium and up to the Edhrine. The Edhrine handed Joseph his swords. The blades stayed and did not dissipate. The ritual worked.

"Let's leave them to their partying. We'll go back to our day," remarked the Edhrine, gesturing toward all of the Edhormond in the room below the podium. The Edhrine used the glass ball to open the doors, leaving the doors open so the other Edhormond could leave when they finished.

Joseph went to his room, and the Edhrine went to his inner chamber. Joseph examined his new blades. These shortswords would no longer need to be sharpened. The hilts and grips were the same, just made of Edhormond steel. Joseph put away his shortswords and went to his semi-machine crossbow. He studied the bolt bundles and single bolts he had in his pack. He had an idea.

Joseph went back to the Chamber of Meeting. He found the Edhrine standing on his platform, facing the wall. "Greetings," said the Edhrine, without turning around.

"I have a request, Edhrine."

"What is it?"

"I would like an Edhormond quiver. I would like to fill it with crossbow bolt bundles, if that is possible."

"It is."

The Edhrine led Joseph into his inner chamber. There, he knelt before the altar and placed a quiver on it. "This quiver is made of Edhormond leather, a tougher version of the cloth we use. The quiver has been dyed brown, so it will not draw eyes," the Edhrine explained. The Edhrine began his ritual, speaking to the altar. The altar spoke back a few times, and by the time the Edhrine finished, the quiver was full of yellow mist. "This yellow mist can be hidden, as can that of your blades. Will for that to happen, and your blade will disappear or your quiver will appear as a normal, empty quiver. It is an ability of a small number of Edhormond weapons. Remember, though, that you'll need to have an alibi for an empty quiver or a sword hilt without a blade. Nobody walks around with just a hilt." With that, Joseph took his new quiver and returned to his room.

18

Empire of Souls

The Mokror looked at one of her latest creations. It was a massive spider, about two feet tall. The real danger to enemies, though, was on the underside. Spiders were in a pouch, much like a kangaroo's pouch, which took up the space on the underside. Most would call this creature a disgusting abomination, but it was a deadly weapon. If killed, spiders ejected out the front from the opening of the pouch.

The Mokror looked at her other creation. Unlike many of her creations, it was not a spider. It was made of human body parts pieced together and brought to life. The creation was not a zombie, however, because the consciences of the body parts' previous owners were not in this new creation. Like the Mokror's spiders and spider carriers, it had a completely new mind. Because it was a human, it could function as an infiltrator, if the skin was covered. However, because the pieces had been sitting in the Mokror's quarters for about a century, the skin was very rotten.

The Ifloract examined his new soldiers. All eight of them were the same. Each one was a flame, at least for now. The new creations floated around the Ifloract, unarmed. "Let the test begin!" shouted the Ifloract. From all sides, ashen soldiers and living flames did all they could to kill the creations. However, the new creations were more powerful than the Ifloract's army thought. One morphed into and ashen soldier and hid among the ranks. He made a small dagger appear and used it against the ashen soldiers. Another conjured a moste and fired, and dropped it into the lava after firing. He conjured another and fired, discarding it only to summon another. This allowed the bodyguard to fire damaging moste shots in rapid succession. The other bodyguards created shields and blades and used them as weapons, occasionally morphing or using another tactic to stay alive. "End the test!" shouted the Ifloract. "This creation has passed!" The creations morphed back into flames and surrounded the Ifloract, facing outward.

The Marantaur stood in the stone chamber. The room was large, with an altar at one end. On the altar lay a dead Edhormond. Crowds of souls lined the sides of the room. He bellowed, "Come! Initiate him!" A soul went to the dead Edhormond lying on the altar. The soul reached into the corpse and pulled. Out of the Edhormond body came a new soul, which screeched in pain. The Marantaur began the next part of the ritual. "Soul, I anoint you as the High General of my militia, but more importantly, the Emperor of the Souls! Serve me well!"

The soul stopped screeching. He sat up, then stood. The Eye of the Edhrine surveyed the part of his new army in the chamber. In a cold, sinister, voice, he spoke, "I will serve you well, as the souls will serve their Emperor! I am no longer the Eye of the Edhrine. I am the Darkest One. That is what you shall call me!"

The Edhrine felt a ripple. At first, it was small, like something slight just happened, but then it clouded the Edhrine's senses and felt like a thundering boom in his ears, a blur in his eyes, and a lack of feeling. The Edhrine recovered to find that he had collapsed on his platform.

A nearby Edhormond asked, "Sir, are you okay?"

"Something very bad just happened, and I need my most elite soldiers here, now!"

Joseph entered the room. A few Edhormond spearmen and archers ran in beside him. Joseph sat, alongside some of the Edhormond, while other Edhormond stood around the table. The Edhrine stood on his platform.

"What happened?" Joseph asked.

The Edhrine spoke, "An important Edhormond has just done something terrible. He has betrayed me. I need you to figure out who. I know of the only few Edhormond who could cause such a ripple in sorcery if they betrayed. Bring them here."

Joseph walked back into the room after rounding up the Edhormond whom he was sent to retrieve. Two elite Edhormond marched behind him, prodding in the last of the Edhormond.

"What is going on?" asked the last one.

The Edhrine explained, "One of you has betrayed me. I called on these men to help me figure out which one of you. Please sit." The Edhormond all sat and the Edhrine began questioning, "You are the Director of Troop Production. You command the mines. If you have betrayed, the ripple would be great, because you could do much damage. Did you?"

"No, Edhrine," the director responded.

"Let's see if you're lying," the Edhrine said, producing a small knife. "This is not torture, but sorcery. I will need a sliver of your flesh. If you're the traitor, step forward to save everyone and yourself the discomfort." Nobody stood. The Edhrine proceeded to use the knife to carve a sliver of stone flesh from each Edhormond. The Edhormond did not feel pain, but they didn't like seeing slices of themselves removed.

The Edhrine finished his interrogation, and left the room. He returned a few minutes later and said, "None of you have betrayed me, but that means it is much worse than I thought. I believe that an important dead Edhormond has risen as a soul. He did not betray me, but rather, he is under another's control. I had a special connection with the Eye, as he was the second-in-command. The ripple was too great for it to be a long-dead Edhormond. The Eye is risen. But, for that ripple, he must have done something terrible or committed to something terrible. Because there are no reports of massacres or any other tragic moves by the enemy, I believe that he received a high rank among the souls, from the Marantaur."

Joseph, the Edhrine, and several Edhormond embarked on another trip, traveling by wagon. It was a civilian-looking wagon, borrowed from the North Morhor Military. A man in civilian clothes sat in the front. The wagon was far into enemy territory by now and nearing its destination. Everyone remained silent the whole ride. Edhormond didn't talk unless necessary, the Edhrine included. Joseph stayed silent, too. Once everyone disembarked, Joseph, the Edhrine, and the Edhormond started walking towards the nearby mountains while the driver pitched a tent and positioned a few empty crates nearby. He brought out some more crates, these filled with weapons, and set those down. Using a bench for a desk, he constructed a fake shop. He posted a sign that read: "By order of the Marantaur's Militia, the weapons here are to be moved by appropriate officials only. The property here belongs to the Marantaur's Militia High Command." Now, the wagon had a reason to be there, and for patrolmen not to loot it.

"I assume these are the Dead Mountains," Joseph speculated.

The Edhrine replied, "Yes, they are. The Errorunsai bury their dead here. Each Errorunsin has a huge tomb to bury their ordinary dead, but special individuals receive their own tombs, the Eye included. No Errorunsai knows the location of the others' tombs. One of the only treaties we've ever signed was not to conquer this area, loot the tombs, or block the other Errorunsai from burying their dead. Alright, men. The Eye's tomb is right here. Form a perimeter around the entryway and yell if anything happens. Joseph, you two, and I will go into the tomb."

The Edhormond set up the perimeter while Joseph, the Edhrine, and two Edhormond spearmen went into the darkness of the tomb.

"I was right," said the Edhrine. They had traveled through the short tunnel into the main room. A sepulcher was in the center, but there was no body inside. The Edhrine went to his knees and examined the area. "Someone dragged the corpse. The marks are difficult to see in the darkness, but they lead outside. Someone dragged the body away. Let's see to where," the Edhrine said. "March out and follow the scuff marks!" Soldiers began the process of following the marks.

The group followed the scuff marks to a mountain pass, which narrowed to become a ravine. The ravine made a bend that Joseph could not see around. "We should not go in there," the Edhrine declared. Near the pass and in the ravine were strange stone statues. Some were of Edhormond doing battle. Others were of Sentinels of Monfor. "We signed a treaty never to go in there! I will not break it!"

"Well, the Marantaur has certainly done a great job at not following those treaties! One end of the deal is broken. There's no sense in holding up the other," Joseph replied.

"You don't understand. Joseph, there's a reason that we signed the treaty. Nobody who goes in there ever comes back, and we know why. There is a fortress in there. In ancient times, far earlier than you know, an empire existed there. The empire had an impregnable position inside the mountains. The Dead Mountains are too steep to climb, too strong to mine, and protected by sorcery. The only way through is by way of the ravine maze. The empire was too primitive to understand the sorcery. They thought it was impossible to mine because of the rock, but really it was rock imbued with sorcery. That sorcery was stronger than one would think and was strong enough to possess armies. So, that's what it did. The sorcery took over the empire by possessing the emperor and many soldiers. The sane ones were mostly killed in battle. Some were captured and tortured to death by the possessed, but one man survived it all. That's how the Errorunsai know all this. The possessed empire marched out with a bloodthirsty hate. However, the combined force of the Errorunsai was able to slay them all. None of them surrendered. All of them recklessly charged, and we had to kill every one of those possessed men. From then on, the kingdoms swore never to pass on the knowledge of that place. The Errorunsai swore to make sure nobody got curious about that area and entered. We were the guardians. Everyone with knowledge swore to never go in there, including the Marantaur. Until now, he kept that oath. Since he is possessed, no oath he swears matters. All that matters to him is power." With that, the Edhrine, Joseph, and the Edhormon turned away and went back to the wagon, and they rode back home.

19

Awakened

Back in Edhormon, Joseph thought about that cursed place. He looked through an atlas and found that the ravine maze was called the Dead Maze. On the map, the maze traversed the area, which was barren of any resources. The map indicated locations where wolves and other dangerous predators roamed the area, depicting its inhospitableness. Joseph knew the maze only took up part of the area, but the atlas used this description to keep people away, and with good reason. The Dead Plain was located north of the maze, and it was there that the sorcery really consumed someone. Joseph knew that sorcery was always the action of an altar, and in turn the one who requested the action. For one to be able to possess others, he wielded considerable power. For him to create an area barren of anything but evil, his power was greater than all Errorunsai combined. However, if there was sorcery, there was a source. If there was a physical object or altar as the source, it could be destroyed. The magic could be reverted. Then again, you had to get to it, wherever it was, and not get possessed along the way. Also, if the Marantaur had his forces there, then a large army would be defending the place. One would have to make it through the maze without dying as a result of lack of resources or by defenders, cross the plain without dying to armies or getting possessed, find the source, and destroy it. That wasn't going to happen very easily.

Joseph heard his door open, and he turned around. An Edhormond messenger announced, "The Edhrine wants you in the Chamber of Meeting." Once the messenger left, Joseph put his atlas in his wagon. He got up and went outside the gate to the Maze of Edhormon. Joseph went to the secret entryway in the side of the mountain, the one that only those who had passed the maze new about. He pulled the entryway open and ascended the stairs behind the door. The door closed behind him. Two Edhormond stood guard at the top of the staircase. Joseph passed them without a word, and went to the Chamber of Meeting.

Joseph sat down at the Edhrine's table. "Welcome," the Edhrine said. "I have called you to assign you a mission."

"What is the mission?" Joseph asked.

"It appears the Marantaur is making a very bold move—too bold for my liking. He is sending a huge army to the area south of the Centaur Woods. He knows that we have defenses there. I do not like this. He has a trick up his sleeve. Therefore, I have sent three legions of Edhormond soldiers to that area. Knowing the souls, they have something really powerful on their side, so you need to go as well."

"Very well." Joseph went down to his room, packed his wagon, and set off with Anvil.

"Go! Go! Go!" directed a soldier. Joseph stepped out of his landing craft. Around him, New Sorwondian soldiers rushed on to the beaches. Ahead, smoke billowed into the sky and fire illuminated the ground. New Sorwondian forces had burned some enemy catapults and battering rams, while the enemy had burned a few of the defenses. Joseph rushed up the shore of the Sacred River and went into the nearest bunker. Inside, a New Sorwondian general was hunched over a map with two orderals.

Joseph walked up to the table and greeted the general. He scanned the map, and said, "Send some men from this bunker over to this brush. Have them fire on the enemies. While the enemies are distracted and putting up their shields, archers atop the bunkers will pick off the men."

"Yes, sir," acknowledged the general. Turning to the orderals, "You heard him! Go!"

With that, Joseph went to one of the bunkers from which archers would fire. He pulled out his semi-machine crossbow and prepared to fire shots at the enemy. Joseph saw the soldiers in the brush. They drew back arrows and fired. As Joseph had anticipated, the enemy began to rotate their formation to block arrows from the brush. While they were moving, the archers around Joseph rained arrows upon them.

Out of nowhere, a gray mist descended upon the battlefield. "What is going on?" shouted a New Sorwondian soldier. The militia men and the souls, however, had perfect visibility. New Sorwondians fell from an overwhelming number of arrows and moste shots.

Joseph ran into a bunker, where there was no mist. Inside, there was a ballista and two soldiers. They could not see out of the hole in the front, and therefore could not fire effectively. Two souls jumped into the bunker. They were skirmishers, carrying two shortswords. The skirmishers killed the two soldiers and cornered Joseph. Joseph backed up, feigning fear, and then lunged, impaling both of the souls. The usual screech and blowing of mist were followed by a deafening boom. The bunker collapsed around Joseph. Joseph ran out the door. Outside, the mist had cleared up, and Joseph encountered something he would never forget. The Eye, in soul form, stood in front of the army of souls and militia men. Unlike the other souls, though, the Eye was more realistic. Parts of him were non-transparent, unlike the usual gray mist. His color, though, was gray. Joseph looked at the visor of his helmet. It did not emit yellow mist, or gray mist, for that matter. There was only a consuming black that reflected no light. "Well, hello there," snickered the Eye, in a cold, dead voice.

Joseph ran to his wagon, and the Anvil steered away from the field. Dead New Sorwondians were piled up everywhere. Stones from catapults buried the bunkers. "Get us out of here!" Joseph shouted.

"The Eye lives," Joseph confirmed. He was standing up, speaking to the Edhrine and several Edhormond who sat around the table. "I saw him. He is extremely powerful. He blinded our men, but none of his. They shot at us until none were left. I fled with Anvil, and we barely escaped with our lives. Anvil got shot by a moste in the arm and is recovering in one of the recovery rooms."

"This is grave news. Go to the recovery ward and check on Anvil. We have much to discuss," the Edhrine said. As Joseph left the room, the Edhrine and the Edhormond began discussing the matter.

Anvil was in the recovery room on his bed when Joseph arrived. His arm recovered, by the looks of it. "How did the procedure go?" Joseph asked.

"It went well. They used a dagger to remove the projectile from my arm and healed it using sorcery." Anvil sat up and continued, "What did the Edhrine say about the report?"

"Good question. He is discussing the matter with some Edhormond now." Anvil stood, and the two left the room.

They went back to their quarters. The wagon was in the center, and a single bed was in the corner. Edhormond did not sleep, so Anvil did not require a bed. Anvil just stood there, like Edhormond did. Joseph didn't understand it. How did they not get bored of just standing? They also didn't eat. Joseph did not ask about that. He snapped back to the present and made meal rations for himself. A few minutes later, the door opened. A messenger entered and said, "The Edhrine has requested both of you." The messenger left after giving the message. Joseph grabbed his weapons, put them on his belt, and left his quarters with Anvil following.

Joseph entered the Chamber of Meeting. The Edhrine was on his platform, looking at the wall. The Edhormond from before were still in their seats. "I have grave news," the Edhrine announced. "New Sorwond has fallen." Joseph was stunned. The entire nation he had raised, the order that had started as a rebellion, and became a major military power, had fallen. The defenses had failed. "Every wall and bunker were wrecked at once," the Edhrine said, "by the Eye."

"How did he take them all out at once?" Joseph asked.

"He used sorcery to create a wave of flames. He had a sort of altar. The average sorcerer could bring down a fort with it, but he did far worse."

"So, now we know the Eye does not require an altar of the purest gold to inflict that much damage," Joseph observed.

"There were no survivors," the Edhrine said glumly.

"How? Hundreds of thousands of people lived in New Sorwond. Not just soldiers, but many civilians, too. None of them survived?"

"That is correct. Every one of them burned in a tidal wave of fire. Fire engulfed the entire Centaur Woods, and the Eye made a smaller wave near Sorwond City. He sent soldiers to kill the few survivors. Edhormond barges saw the survivors, but could not make it to shore in time."

20

Fire and Water

With New Sorwond falling, fear would spread through the southern areas. This fear could convince those areas to betray the Three. Joseph knew that if one of the Three died, then this fear would consume them, to the point of madness. He thought the Mokror would be the first to fall since she only had her spiders as an army. Yes, the spiders were effective, but only when combined with other types of troops. Joseph knew that he had to convince the Edhrine and the Ifloract to shore up the Mokror's defenses.

Joseph did not have a hard time convincing the Edhrine and Ifloract. The Edhrine sent his steel and Ifloract brought troops. Edhormond moved materials off the barges and onto Mokror's island. Joseph watched as they moved off blocks of Edhormond steel as others stacked them up. Edhormond sorcerers used a spell to covert the stacks of blocks into a solid wall. On the top of the wall, workers added railings and cover for archers.

The Ifloract's troops stood in rank and file. The living flames floated in perfect formation above the halberds. Joseph saw the Ifloract in conversation with a living flame with several other living flames surrounding him. Those must have been bodyguards or something. Joseph approached the Ifloract. The two exchanged greetings, and the living flame to which the Ifloract was talking departed towards the army. The guards around the Ifloract morphed into ashen soldiers and conjured obsidian swords.

Joseph asked the Ifloract, "What are those things?"

"They are my new bodyguards. I made them in the Depths of Flame. They can morph into certain forms and conjure various things, such as weapons. They are my elite. I plan to make more, to do certain...assignments for me."

"What kind of assignments?"

"Well, maybe putting the Eye to rest, killing the Marantaur and burning his body, so we do not have to deal with the Marantaur's soul, and other things along the lines of that."

While the Mokror's island was fortified, sinister plans were being set in motion.

"Darkest One, I give you orders," the Marantaur said to the Eye.

"What shall they be?"

"You have done well. The Destruction of New Sorwond shall be remembered forever as a tragedy among the Three, but a victory among us. Now, do the same to the Elemental Mountains. Target the Depths of Flame. Flood it with water, and drown the Ifloract's personal army."

"It will be done," replied the Eye, the Emperor of the Souls.

The Marantaur went into the deepest cavern under the Dead Fortress. There, he went to the Throne of the Dead. Upon it sat the former Emperor of the Souls.

"Why do you come to me?" the emperor asked.

"I have come to do this!" The Marantaur threw one of

his maces and killed the emperor. Now, the Marantaur had complete control over the souls. It was no longer an allied nation, but a nation under him. The Marantaur retrieved his mace. He noticed some gray mist surrounding the base of the throne. Suddenly, it hit him. This throne was the source, the altar, which rose the first soul. It was the great source of evil, and it had to be guarded. The Marantaur looked at the throne again. It was too small for him, so he figured the Eye could sit upon it. Also, the Marantaur could not fail as the emperor did. The emperor taught the Marantaur too much, and had no way to control him. The Marantaur knew how to drain power from objects because of the emperor, and the Marantaur learned from the emperor's mistakes. He would not reveal all his secrets at once.

The Eye silently moved toward the depths. Behind him trailed a soul of a horse, which was pulling a water-filled wagon. The Eye shot the two guards watching the gate. The Ifloract made a fatal flaw in his design. His fortress went ever deeper underground. Water from the surface would eventually reach the Ifloract's personal lava pool, and flood the entire place. A wagon full of water would do a lot of damage. The Eye motioned to the souls who accompanied him to begin dumping water from the wagon. Once empty, the Eye summoned for a second wagon. He continued filling the Depths of Flame with water until he heard a familiar sound. He heard the clanking of the Edhormond soldiers. This was most unpleasant.

An Edhormond general marched at the head of the army. The soldiers of the Ifloract in the Depths of Flame used the Connection to call for help. The Edhrine assigned this particular Edhormond army to put an end to the Eye's little flood.

The Eye saw them coming. "Kill them!" commanded the

Eye. A horde of souls charged the Edhormond. The souls and Edhormond clashed and tore at each other, while the wagons continued to dump water. The souls were sufficiently delaying the Edhormond. He would get all of the water in, and flood enough of the Depths of Flame to cause a big problem for the Ifloract.

The Edhormond general surveyed the battle and realized the Eye was employing a delay tactic. "Send in the elites!" the general ordered. From the back of the army came eight living flames of the Ifloract. The flames enlarged and levitated over the souls. Arrows came up from the crowd, but the flames dodged them.

The Eye saw the new force coming. He saw the living flames grow larger, and he felt an emotion he had never felt since his death: fear. "Kill those flames!" the Eye commanded. Souls fired mostes, but to no avail. The flames dove down and consumed the wagons, and water gushed out. The Eye had to resort to his personal abilities. Gray fog descended upon the field. The Edhormond general could not see. Arrows flew. The general's army was in total confusion.

"Hold formation!" the general shouted. "Raise shields!" The soldiers returned into formation and blocked the arrows with shields. The Edhormond reached the location of the wagons, but there were no wagons there. There was nothing.

The Eye cackled loudly, enough for the whole Edhormond army to hear. "You have won this round, but I guarantee that it will be a different story when I return!" With that, the Eye fled into the South Morhor Mountains.

The Ifloract finished garrisoning the Mokror's island, only to learn that the Eye's next target was his very own base. Luckily, an Edhormond army defeated them with the help of his new specialized soldiers. The Ifloract thought of what to call them as they were still nameless. He decided to call them the Guardians of the Flame.

The Connection saved the Ifloract's base. When it was constructed all those millennia ago, the Ifloract did not like the idea of it, but now it saved his base. The Connection was a passageway that connected the four Errorunsai. Its tunnels intersected in the northern half of the world. The passageways had periodic support beams, and a wooden floor. The floor was imbued with sorcery, and it was essentially, one big, underground altar with a part near each Errorunsin. It revolved around a loophole in the mechanics of altars. A sorcerer could make anything levitate above an altar, even if no sorcery can be done with the object. One can also make said object go to any point on the altar with just a thought. With a huge altar like the Connection, each Errorunsin could also send things across the world, such as messages or supplies. The passageways were too small for armies, though, and the Errorunsai had many defenses to prevent surprise attacks such as spikes to block anything that is the size of a soldier from entering. The Ifloract's soldiers used the Connection to send the Edhrine a note, and the Edhormond army came. The Ifloract realized that the Connection was a powerful tool that could bolster any Errorunsin's defenses. It was also a vulnerability. If the Marantaur got in there, he could dismantle the spikes and other defenses, enabling his troops to raid any Errorunsai's base. The Connection had to be defended.

The Ifloract posted many guards, and even operated an outpost at the intersection. Sending supplies was easy because of the Connection's transportation ability. There were regular patrols that guarded the passageways, and spiked barriers blocked the passageway that led towards the North Morhor Plain. Although the Marantaur blocked that end of the passage, there was no telling if he planned on returning. The Ifloract returned to his base by way of the Connection. He went to his lava pool and fabricated a large shard of obsidian with a message inscribed in it, describing to the Edhrine and the Mokror the underground defenses he placed. He would send it first to the Edhrine, and then the Edhrine would send it to the Mokror.

An Edhormond messenger approached the Edhrine, who was standing on his platform facing the wall. The Edhrine sensed the messenger's presence and asked, "What is your message?" The messenger placed a large obsidian shard on the table and left. The Edhrine picked up the shard and read the inscription. He used a glass sphere in the room to summon another messenger. When the messenger came in, the Edhrine said to him, "Use the Connection to send this to the Mokror."

The Edhrine walked out of the Chamber of Meeting and traversed the hallways. He ended up on one of the many bridges that went over the mines, where Edhormond workers carved humanoid statues. He moved along and took a few staircases to a storage area. In it were roughly a hundred thousand lifeless statues and two Edhormond on patrol. The Edhrine descended some steps. This room served as an altar upon which all statues were placed. "Clear the altar!" ordered the Edhrine. The two patrolmen marched out and flanked the Edhrine. The Edhrine concentrated. This altar had a rune imbued in it, so it could only perform that spell. No words were required and the statues began moving. Then, they marched through a doorway into another room. The Edhrine left the room, and the two patrolmen followed him.

The Edhrine continued walking until he reached a huge room.

He stood on a balcony, and thousands of Edhormond remained motionless in the room, holding their spears and shields. An Edhormond general was also on the balcony, directing the activities of soldiers. Seeing the Edhrine, the general began to step aside, but the Edhrine motioned him back. The Edhrine did not have any orders. He was just there to see how things were going. After watching the Garrison Hall from the balcony for a while, the Edhrine moved to a different room. This one was smaller, but still huge. Here, the Edhormond did not possess armor nor weapons. They simply stood at attention with their hands empty. This was the Hall of Initiates, where Edhormond who had not yet been initiated waited for the next session. The Edhrine stepped onto a balcony in the Hall of Initiates, where two Edhormond stood on the balcony with their armor and weapons. "The next Ritual of Initiation draws near. Prepare yourselves," the Edhrine announced. With that, the Edhrine left, and the two Edhormond on the balcony followed him. The Edhrine went to the Hall of Arms and gave the new soldiers their weapons. Of course, the yellow mist parts did not appear when they picked up the equipment. They had yet to be initiated. From there, they went to the Hall of Initiation where the Edhrine initiated them.

Joseph returned from the Mokror's island. The fortification was complete. However, the Eye attacked the Ifloract's caves, which were not fortified. At least the attack was repelled. He was thinking, when a messenger opened the door to his room and announced, "The Edhrine requests you in the Chamber of Meeting."

Joseph and Anvil arrived and sat. The Edhrine turned around and faced them. "Greetings."

"Greetings. What is the issue?" Joseph asked.

"The Eye did not take a hint from his recent defeat," the Edhrine explained.

"He is attacking again?" Joseph asked.

"Yes, he is. I am sending you and more Edhormond than you will ever need. You will have three hundred thousand men. That should be enough for the Eye to take a hint."

Joseph rode on an Edhormond steel catapult. A hundred Edhormond soldiers pushed the catapult, which was more than enough to make the catapult and Joseph a light load. As the army neared the Depths of Flame, Joseph stared in shock. The army had arrived, but too late. The Elemental Mountains were leveled. There was nothing left. The Ifloract's soldiers tried to run away, but none survived. Moste souls fired at them. A few times, a wave of ashen soldiers charged away, but each time, moste shots slayed them. More shocking, though, was the collapse of the Depths of Flame. The mountains were somehow brought down, and that collapsed the Depths. "Finish off these souls!" Joseph shouted. The Edhormond charged forward, except for the archers and soldiers manning the catapults. Still, the souls were already leaving. They had done what they had come to do, and took the souls out of many of the ashen soldiers' corpses. "Pull back!" Joseph shouted. There was no sense wasting troops by pursuing them into land crawling with souls and militia soldiers.

21

The New Empire

The Eye sat upon his new throne. It was stone, dead stone. The Marantaur told the Eye how to consume power inside of objects, but he withheld some knowledge. The Eye could not become as powerful as the Marantaur without knowing more. "Bring me the Marantaur, but make sure he is missing his arms and legs!" the Eye ordered.

The Marantaur stood atop the Dead Fortress, when he felt a sharp pain in his left leg. He turned to find the soul of a Nacreato skirmisher had just cut off that leg. Another skirmisher approached and removed his arms. With only one leg, the Marantaur could do little as the first skirmisher removed his other leg. The skirmishers dragged the Marantaur to the Chamber of the Throne. "Why have you betrayed me?" the Marantaur asked when he realized the Eye had ordered this. "I could give you so much more power!"

"That is right. You can, and you will," the Eye sneered.

A skirmisher raised his blade to decapitate the Marantaur.

"I cannot give you power if I am nonexistent!" the Marantaur protested.

"No, but death is not the end. You and your militia will join my army! You will be under my control, and so will your knowledge!"

The Marantaur screamed, and fell silent as a skirmisher separated his head from his body. The Eye rose from his throne and, with the help of the two skirmishers, removed the Marantaur's soul from his body. Immediately, the new soul began writhing in pain. The Eye knew that the other souls would feel this pain until they were completely loyal to him. He was the only one who would never feel this pain. He was always loyal to himself, was he not?

All around the Dead Fortress, militia men were killed. They returned as souls, and helped convert the others. Soon the souls killed every living thing throughout their land. The Eye gave orders to his souls, "Prepare an army to march upon Edhormon."

The Edhrine sat in the Chamber of Meeting with his generals. He knew that the Eye would be coming for Edhormon sooner or later. Either they would come to Edhormon first and the southlands second, or the southlands first and Edhormon second. Either way, things were going badly. The Edhrine thought about the secret weapon hidden in the runes on the wall. He could try to use it, but the risk was enormous. It would undo the very existence of sorcery. The souls would disappear, but so would the Edhrine and each Errorunsin. The Edhormond would be erased from the world, and in a painful way. Sorcery would be gone, but any sorcerers would be killed, and they would forever be forgotten.

The Eye watched as the armies of souls marched onto their new weapon. It was a massive barge, which plunged into the sea below and into darkness. It had siege weapons and armories that rivaled Edhormon. The Marantaur constructed it a long time ago in preparation for this moment, and the Eye brought it out from its hiding place. Killing the Marantaur was a great decision. This barge was one of many good things that had come from it.

A soul informed the Eye that everyone was onboard, and the Eye ordered them to take off. Souls untied the ropes securing the barge to the shore. The barge was wooden, but it had the design of Edhormond barges, with oars sticking out of the walls. The barge was square, similar to an Edhormond barge. However, it was about fifty times the size of one of those. The souls began rowing. With that, the nameless barge set off for Edhormon.

An Edhormond soldier and archers looked from a watch tower. An archer sensed something bad was about to happen. Then, it came into view. A humongous barge that was comparable to the size of Sorwond City. It was the souls, and they were coming for Edhormon.

Edhormon bustled with activity. Archers got to the walls and soldiers to the gates. The Edhrine stood on a bridge watching soldiers running through the mines to other hallways and rooms. The mines were not just mines. Some parts were well-traveled intersections and bridges. The Edhrine sensed someone behind him and whirled around to find a messenger. "Sir, the other Errorunsai have arrived and appear to have brought another ally," the messenger said.

The Edhrine walked into the sitting room to find the other Errorunsai there. Through a window, he saw the spiders and ashen soldiers marching into the halls of Edhormon. Then, the Edhrine spotted a Sentinel to the left of them. "Seize him!" the Edhrine shouted.

Two Edhormond pounced onto the Sentinel and pinned him

to the floor.

"Stop!" the Ifloract shouted. "We recruited them to help us. They are not souls, and they are making wooden defenses outside, so they will not be in your fortress, Edhrine. They have sworn to be at peace with the Edhormon until the last soul is dead again.

"Very well," the Edhrine said, and he had the Edhormond release the Sentinel.

A thunderstorm rolled over Edhormon as the raft drew within range. Catapults built by the Sentinels threw a volley. The barge responded with its own. The Siege of Edhormon had begun as the barge drew closer, launching stones from catapults. The barge reached the shore and the Sentinels retreated backwards. It was so massive that it barely took any damage from the Sentinels' stones. Ten ramps on the front of the barge lowered and hordes of souls rushed off while the barge's catapults fired on Edhormon.

The Eye studied the battle. As well as it was going, he felt the need to speed up the whole war. If his troops reached the Labyrinth of Edhormon, the southern nations would join him out of fear. When those nations think they have saved themselves, his souls would crush them, and his army would grow. Then, they could come to Edhormon and finish off the Errorunsai.

The souls' envoy stood in the meeting room in Mohraight's capital and convinced them to join. Nacreato was next. When these two large nations were on the Eye's side, the rest of the south would surrender or die. The envoy left the Mohraight capital city and went to Nacreato. The envoy convinced Nacreato to join, too. As soon as these two joined, all of the smaller nations joined out of fear, except for Traste. Traste's failure to join the souls led to its crushing defeat. Forces from the other southern nations wiped out Traste and the souls added the fallen to their armies. The souls ordered Mohraight and Nacreato to wipe out the other nations of the south, and the souls rose them as well. With only Nacreato and Mohraight left, the souls of all the other nations of the south crushed them. Now, only Edhormon remained. The army of souls now numbered in the millions, and every soul was aboard the enormous barge, or on the land fighting against the defenders. Things were going very well for the Eye.

The Edhrine stood beside the Edhormond archers in the battlements above the gate to the Labyrinth of Edhormon. "Aim for the ones approaching the town! We need to make the ambush convincing!" the Edhrine told the Edhormon. Before the siege, the Edhrine had ordered men to hide in the buildings of the town. The citizens relocated to a safe room within Edhormon. Now, he just had to get the souls to take the bait, which was not difficult. The Eye would want to kill all those people to strengthen his army. Little did the Eye know, the people would fight back.

The souls marched deep into the town and the trap was sprung. The Edhrine knew that the Eye would have thrice as many souls marching in from the southlands, but each soul slain counted towards a victory. A victory, the Edhrine sensed, which would come eventually. These souls would not last forever. Even if this war was lost, the Edhrine could still defeat the souls within the next five-thousand years. He just hoped he could win now and save some of humanity.

The Ifloract stood beside the Sentinels. "Release my troops!" he ordered. One of his bodyguards went to the Labyrinth of Edhormon and opened the gate. Out poured every ashen soldier and living flame of the Ifloract. They charged forward and engaged the souls in melee combat. Even the ones who guarded the Connection came to fight, because the Connection had been collapsed intentionally. The Errorunsai no longer needed it since the Errorunsai were all in Edhormon. It was also a vulnerability, considering how the souls could easily march through it. Therefore, the Errorunsai transferred the guards to Edhormon and forever buried the Connection.

The Mokror sat in the pouch of one of her spider carriers. Around her were various spiders and some of the zombie-like creations. The Mokror was ejected from the pouch along with everyone else inside of it. She whirled around to find ten arrows in the spider carrier's face. She ran forward and decided to forget about riding in a carrier. Ahead of her was the soul army and a battle that would be decided by who had the better soldiers. One army against another, with no ambushes or traps left that the Errorunsai had to offer. It was the Eye's move.

The Eye looked at the battle from his barge. The Errorunsai seemed to have no more surprises, but he remained cautious. He could see the Edhormond Mountains in front of him. Edhormon lurked within those mountains, and he was determined to conquer it. The Eye telepathically communicated with his souls. He told them to go straight for the gate, and ignore all distractions.

The Edhrine sensed a change in the souls' actions. The souls were no longer fighting. Rather, they were running towards the Gate of the Labyrinth of Edhormon without a care about the soldiers around them. The Edhrine was prepared for the Eye's move. "Raise the walls!" Wood panels on the ground, disguised as random debris, flipped upward to form a wall. The souls ran face-first into the wall and Edhormond thrusted their spears through holes in the wall to put those souls to rest. This did not work for long however, as souls climbed on top of each other and jumped over the wall.

The Eye surveyed the battle. There were the two sides, the Errorunsai and the souls. A border separated them where weapons clashed and bodies fell, only to be risen as souls. There was also a long, thin stretch of land covered by souls scrambling to the Gate of Edhormon. The Eye told a soul next to him, "I said EVERY soul should charge the gate! Not just these ones!" The soul scrambled down and ordered all souls to charge. With that, every soul in the army mindlessly charged towards the gate into the ranks of the Errorunsai.

The Mokror surveyed the battle from a small wooden tower erected by the Sentinels. The souls charged forward, senselessly colliding with the Sentinels, ashen soldiers, and Edhormond in the front. They rampaged through the ranks, cutting soldiers in half left and right. "Retreat!" the Mokror ordered. "Retreat to Edhormon!" With that, the soldiers ran with shields behind them. They entered into the Labyrinth of Edhormon and the gate shut behind them. The Mokror ran in last along with the Ifloract. Some Edhormond guards finished off the few souls who managed to squeeze into the Labyrinth of Edhormon before the gate closed.

The Errorunsai and Joseph met up in a hallway. Through the windows, Joseph saw the legions of souls raising shields to block arrows and firing back at Edhormond archers and living flames. They waited for the Eye's next command. Joseph had been within the ranks of soldiers throughout the battle. He had been doing what he did best, killing souls. The Errorunsai were better commanders than him, so he left that to them and joined the ranks as an elite skirmisher.

"There is little to say. The Siege of Edhormon has truly begun. We are trapped in the fortress, and the enemy surrounds us. Our only hope is to continue to kill the souls until there are none left. We cannot win this fight in a conventional manner. We have almost every disadvantage. There are more of them, they have a great strategist leading them, and they have us trapped. I am afraid, however, that we have no other option but to fight to the last soldier and hope enough survivors remain to harass the souls for another few years. Maybe, then, the Eye's reign will be over," the Edhrine told those present. Nobody had anything to say, so everyone went back to the battlements.

The Edhrine peered out a window and saw the ram. Crowds of souls parted and through the gap came a battering ram more massive than anything the Edhrine had ever seen, and the Edhrine had seen a lot. The ram advanced, and the souls on board pulled the huge pole back. They let go and the pole swung and hit the gate with a thunderous crash. Fragments of the gate flew in many directions. Souls poured in through the hole. The Edhrine was stunned. That ram just destroyed an Edhormond steel gate in one strike. That was impressive. The Edhrine recovered from the shock and ordered troops to intercept the souls and defend the Labyrinth of Edhormon.

The souls poured into the Labyrinth and pushed back the defenders. In the chaos, a crowd of souls slew the Ifloract, and his bodyguards fell one by one as well. The souls poured into the main fortress, and here the Mokror fell, pummeled by arrows and moste shots. The Edhrine, Joseph, and a few survivors of the battle assembled in a room. They blocked the door in case a soul found the room because souls were searching the fortress, looking for the survivors.

"Joseph," the Edhrine said.

"Yes?"

"I possess a secret weapon. Inside the Chamber of Meeting there are those runes I carved in the wall. They are imbued with a powerful spell that only Errorunsai can enact. It will erase all sorcery from the world. The souls will be gone, the Eye will be gone, and all creations of sorcery will be gone. All surviving Edhormond will be gone, as will remaining ashen soldiers, living flames, and the Mokror's creations. However, that is not all. I will be gone. Now, I am willing to make that sacrifice to end the souls, but are you?"

"I am willing to make that sacrifice." Joseph would no longer enjoy his Edhormond blades, but that was a small sacrifice compared to giving up the Edhrine. Unfortunately, though, there was no other way.

"Okay, we must reach the Chamber of Meeting at all costs."

The Edhrine, Joseph, and the survivors snuck down the hallway toward the Chamber of Meeting. They took out two patrol squads, but they were not sure if those souls could telepathically communicate the situation to the Eye. Either way, they continued moving. The group dwindled to just the Edhrine and Joseph. Joseph was one of the last surviving humans. He was sure that some humans were hiding in the southlands or even in New Sorwond, and he would survive after the spell.

The Edhrine opened the door to the Chamber of Meeting and Joseph quickly shot all of the souls inside with a machine crossbow he took from an armory. The Edhrine ran to his platform and knelt, beginning the ritual. The runes on the wall began to glow yellow. Joseph turned and stood guard until a loud crash startled him. He whirled around and saw that a boulder crushed the wall with the runes and pinned the Edhrine beneath the rubble. Joseph heard footsteps behind him and whirled back around. Six Edhormond souls marched in and formed a shield wall. Behind them was the Eye.

"I see there is but one survivor, and he shall not survive," the Eye announced.

"Do you remember when we fought against the Marantaur together?" Joseph asked, attempting to bring the Eye back to his original self.

The Eye appeared to go deep into thought, and then suddenly threw his spear, piercing Joseph. Joseph fell to his knees, and then to the floor. He was dead. "Give me his soul!" the Eye commanded. The six Edhormond souls reached into Joseph and pulled out his soul. Joseph was overcome with pain as all souls were, until he was completely loyal to the Eye.

Glossary

Centaur: An evil race of half-horse, half-man creatures native to the Centaur Woods.

Centaur Woods: Woods east of Sorwond where the Centaurs lived.

Connection: A large altar that allowed the Errorunsai to send messages and supplies to each other.

Dark Mountains: Mountains made impregnable by ancient sorcery, and were where the Errorunsai buried their dead.

Dead Fort: A fortress within the Dead Plain that was once home to an ancient empire.

Dead Maze: A maze of meandering, narrow ravines within the Dead Mountains that led to the Dead Plain.

Dead Plain: A plain filled with evil sorcery, where long ago an ancient empire fell.

Depths of Flame: Home of the Ifloract and his army, situated in the Mountains of the Elements.

Edhormon: An underground Edhormond fortress set within the mountains of the same name.

Edhormond: Stone soldiers based from Edhormon; of or relating to Edhormon.

Edhormond Runes: An arithmetic system used by the Edhormond.

Edhormond Steel: A strong, black steel used by the Edhormond.

Edhrine: The Errorunsin who was the leader of the Edhormond.

Errorunsai: Four long-living, powerful beings who were excellent duelists and powerful sorcerers.

Errorunsin: An individual Errorunsai.

The Eye of the Edhrine: An Edhormond who was once second-in-command to the Edhrine. The Eye was killed and became the Emperor of the Souls.

Handheld Gunpowder Cannon (HGC): The name the New Sorwondians used for the moste.

Joseph: A young man from Sorwond who liberated the nation and fought in the War of the Errorunsai.

Klokar: The evil ruler of the Centaurs.

Klokar's Axe: The heavy axe wielded by Klokar, imbued with sorcery that made its wielder a mighty warrior.

Klokar's Palace: A sprawling palace on the edge of a cliff in the northern Centaur Woods, which later became a city after Klokar's defeat.

Ifloract: The Errorunsin who led an army of ashen soldiers and living flames and lives in the Depth of Flames.

Ifloract's Army: Ashen soldiers and living flames created by the Ifloract.

Marantaur: The Errorunsin who turned out to be the One.

Marantaur's Militia: The army from the South Morhor mountains, which followed the Marantaur.

Mohraight Graveyard: A huge area of rocks located southeast of Edhormon filled with rotting bodies and ships and surrounds the home of the Mokror.

Mokror: The Errorunsin who led legions of spiders and lived on an island in the center of the Mohraight Graveyard

Mokror's Spiders: The giant spiders and other creations created by the Mokror.

Moste: A single-use weapon, developed by Traste, which was capable of piercing heavy armor.

Mountains of the Elements: A mountain range dominated by sorcery, consisting of the Ravine of Air, Valley of Earth, Peak of Frost, and Depths of Flame.

Nations of the Southlands: A collection of nations south of Edhormon that was comprised of Mohraight Kingdom, Nacreato, Monfor, Laste, Traste, Acronomon, Lacon, Zser, Zygyptania, and Ysio.

New Sorwond: The nation formed by Joseph after he liberated Sorwond.

Rebellion of Broken Chains: The rebellion formed by Joseph.

Salo: The King of Sorwond.

Sorwond: A tyrannical kingdom led by Salo, in which Joseph lived.

Souls: Fallen who were risen by sorcery as soldiers of evil.

War of the Errorunsai: A war between the Three and the One that was foretold in the Prophecy of the Errorunsai.